FORTRESS PALOMINO

As the grasslands of War Smoke fill with steers for the coming trail drives, Marshal Matt Fallen wires other lawmen for help in keeping his town peaceful until the drift moves north. Kid Palomino and his sidekick, Red Rivers, heed the call and ride in to help. When they discover that notorious bandit Santiago Del Rosa has crossed the border with his gang, they don't hesitate to leap into action. Can Kid and Rivers stop Santiago before more blood is spilled?

MICHAEL D. GEORGE

FORTRESS PALOMINO

Complete and Unabridged

LINFORD
Leicester

First published in Great Britain in 2012 by
Robert Hale Limited
London

First Linford Edition
published 2014
by arrangement with
Robert Hale Limited
London

A catalogue record for this book is available
from the British Library.

ISBN 978–1–4448–1885–7

Published by
F. A. Thorpe (Publishing)
Anstey, Leicestershire

Set by Words & Graphics Ltd.
Anstey, Leicestershire
Printed and bound in Great Britain by
T. J. International Ltd., Padstow, Cornwall

This book is printed on acid-free paper

Dedicated with thanks to my friend
Sarah Quirke

Prologue

A sickly-sweet mist hung across the canyon as the three riders spurred and drove their horses on. Seasoned lawman Sheriff Race Hawkins and his two deputies Fred Coyle and Steve Kelly had ridden nearly thirty miles on their way from Los Remos to War Smoke and knew that within another few hours they would reach their destination.

As the horsemen reached halfway along the Rio Concho canyon they suddenly realized that there was something ahead of them that was masked by the swirling vapour, which drifted up from the nearby Rio Grande and could hang in the air for days at a time.

Hawkins raised his free hand and dragged his reins up to his gleaming tin star. All three of them came to an abrupt halt and sat watching the dark shadows ahead of them.

'That's riders, Race,' Coyle said knowingly as he held his lathered-up quarter horse in check and tried to pull his rifle from under his saddle fender.

'A lot of riders,' Kelly added drily. He tried to count the mysterious creatures who were blocking the canyon and, therefore, their advance. 'Must be two dozen of the critters by my reckoning.'

'More like thirty,' Hawkins corrected. He drew one of his Colts from its holster and cocked its well-oiled hammer. 'Can your younger eyes make any of them out?'

Coyle felt his upper lip stick to his teeth. 'I can make out sombreros, Race.'

'Could be bandits,' Hawkins guessed. 'We're close to the river border here. This is an easy place for them to cross over.'

'Only one critter is that bold,' Kelly said, as his horse, like its master, became increasingly nervous. 'Santiago.'

Hawkins knew that his deputy was more than likely right. He took a deep breath and licked his dry lips, trying to work out what they should do. There seemed, to his mature mind, to be few options available. To turn and run meant certain death. To advance meant taking on at least thirty riders. His eyes searched all about them for cover. There was none.

'What we gonna do, Race?' Coyle cranked the handguard of his Winchester and sent a spent casing flying over his shoulder.

'Only one thing we can do, Fred.' Hawkins gently tapped his spurs and set his horse walking towards the riders hidden in the fog ahead of them. 'We get as close as we can. Then, if they try anything lethal, we try and kill as many of the varmints as we can.'

It was a crude plan but the only one he could think of.

The closer they got the clearer the small army of horsemen became. Hawkins had been correct. There were over thirty of the sombrero-wearing riders and each of them was holding on to a rifle.

'Damn it all,' Kelly gulped, 'we can't fight this many.'

'We can,' Hawkins whispered.

The phalanx of horseflesh parted and a man, well-known on both sides of the border, nudged his magnificent white stallion to walk out from among his men.

Again the three lawmen drew rein.

'Santiago!' Hawkins gasped.

'It is him,' Kelly agreed.

'We're in big trouble, Race.' Coyle sighed.

'You may go on your way, *amigos*.' Santiago gestured for the three men wearing stars to pass by them, as though he were a king bestowing gifts on his subjects.

The deputies looked at the grim-faced Hawkins. The sheriff returned their glances, nodded at them, then spurred. His men followed suit.

The three riders rode around the group of bandits and aimed their mounts west, for War Smoke.

'Kill them,' Santiago ordered.

The deafening barrage filled the air. Bullets tore into the three men and cut both deputies down from their horses. Droplets of blood floated in the sunshine. Though riddled with countless bullets in his back, Race Hawkins managed to ride on.

1

Huge herds of freshly branded steers had been gathered on the ranges around War Smoke as a new season of cattle drives was about to commence. The sprawling town was overflowing with strangers who had been drawn across the West in the hope that they might get lucky and be hired on for the three-month journey north to the nearest railhead. For towns like War Smoke this was always the most profitable time of the year. During this brief period before the individual drives set out on their arduous journeys the town made ninety per cent of its annual income.

Yet, as with any town swollen with five times more menfolk than it could easily cater for, this was also the most dangerous time of the year. Too many men meant too many guns.

Guns in the hands of strangers who went unrecognized by the men who wore tin stars on their chests made for an uncomfortable few weeks until the wranglers were hired and the herds were started on their way.

It was said that guns were just expensive hammers unless you knew how to handle them. Yet even hammers could be deadly weapons in the hands of those who desired nothing more than causing mayhem. The majority of the drifters who had arrived during the previous few weeks had little knowledge of gunplay but there were others who proudly sported their heavily notched six-shooters in hand-tooled holsters. These men were not looking for low-paid jobs as cowhands; they had other motives for being in War Smoke.

The guns on their hips were deadly and their masters knew how to use them expertly, with lethal precision and speed.

With the town's population multiplied to such dangerous levels and fights breaking out every few hours Marshal Matt Fallen realized that this year he would have to try and hire a few more star-packers to assist his long-time deputy, Elmer Hook, and himself keep the peace until the herds went on their way.

Fallen knew that even though War Smoke was a large town there were few trustworthy souls capable of upholding the law within its boundaries.

By calling in favours to various other lawmen in surrounding towns the marshal had ensured that at least a handful of seasoned deputies would be dispatched to help him and Elmer keep the peace for the next week or so. Fallen had sent out a half-dozen telegraph messages and was satisfied with the positive response from his friends. Deputies would be arriving at any time.

The sun had only just set on the cattle-filled range when the two horse-men steered their horses towards the lights of the bustling town. Unlike all those who had reached War Smoke before them over the previous few weeks, these men had gleaming tin stars pinned to their topcoats. In the dim light of the half-moon the stars gleamed like jewels.

They had ridden fifty miles in answer to Fallen's wire.

The youngest of the pair rode a high-shouldered palomino stallion and went by the handle of Kid Palomino. Few knew his given name, yet most people had heard of him and his prowess with his pair of matched Colt .45s. His saddle pal was a bearded man with thinning crimson hair; he sat astride a buckskin quarter horse and he too hid his true identity behind a nickname. Red Rivers was at least a dozen years older than his companion, but he always followed where the Kid led. Some men were rams and others merely sheep. Some led and others followed. Red Rivers was happy to follow his smarter friend wherever Palomino led him.

In over a score of towns the pair had worked as lawmen. They had answered the call for help sent out by US Marshal Matt Fallen eagerly.

The town of War Smoke was new to them and these men liked to keep moving ever onward to fresh pastures.

The lights had already started to glow out in the darkness ahead of the riders before they stopped their mounts and dropped to the ground. As each second passed War Smoke grew brighter out on the vast range. It was bathed in an almost orange hue and even across the distance between the horsemen and the settlement the sound of pianos reached their ears. Both men stared at the place towards which they were headed.

A wooden signpost had freshly painted lettering on it, declaring the name of the town to anyone who could read.

'We found it, Red,' Palomino said. He hit the dust off his Stetson against his leg. 'War Smoke.'

'Gimme ya hat, Kid,' Red said, reaching across to his partner. He plucked two canteens from his saddle. 'I'll water the nags.'

Kid Palomino tossed his hat to his friend, then rested against the saddle of his sturdy horse. 'Do ya figure we should break out the jerky, or maybe wait until we hit town and then buy ourselves two-inch-thick steaks? Which'll it be?'

Rivers dropped both their hats on the ground and filled their crowns with water. Both horses dropped their necks and began to drink the precious liquid.

'Jerky or steak?' Red smiled and then laughed. 'Damn! That sure is a hard 'un.'

'Steak it is,' the Kid sighed, rubbing a sleeve across his sweat-beaded brow. 'With buttered eggs. Sunny side up.'

Rivers took a mouthful of water, then spat it out. 'We sure found War Smoke in time. This water is mighty sour.'

'Ya ever heard of Matt Fallen, Red?' Palomino asked his pal.

'Nope.'

'I have.' The Kid leaned over and plucked his hat up off the ground. 'I heard tell he's the fastest gun alive.'

'I thought that you was the fastest gun alive, Kid.' Rivers picked up his own hat and placed it on his head. The water droplets felt good as they trickled down his neck.

Kid Palomino ran a gloved hand around the leather hatband inside his Stetson, then placed it on his head. 'I'm fast, but I heard that Fallen is faster. I sure ain't hankering to test the theory, though.'

'How old is he?'

'Thirty something.'

'Hell. He must be real fast with his gun to be a lawman and live that long.' Rivers smiled and hung the canteens on the saddle horn. Then he raised his left leg and poked his boot into his stirrup. 'How old are you nowadays?'

Palomino raised his eyebrows and gathered up his reins. 'I'm a little shy of thirty.'

'Then I figure ya gotta be almost as

fast as him.' Rivers watched his pal spring upward until the pointed toe of his boot found the stirrup. 'Why're we here again?'

'Fallen needs extra deputies, Red,' Palomino explained. His stallion shook its creamy white mane as it stared at the distant town. 'War Smoke gets mighty dangerous this time of the year. Leastways, that's what I heard.'

'Anything to do with all these steers?' Rivers pointed at the thousands of head of beef on the hoof that surrounded them under the rising half-moon.

'Kinda.' Palomino leaned forward and whispered into his horse's ear. 'C'mon, Nugget. Let's go find a real old lawman and ask him for a job.'

As the palomino thundered away the older rider spurred his quarter horse into action and galloped after his friend.

The two horsemen aimed their mounts at the now well-illuminated town. The closer they got to War Smoke the more they noticed the familiar sound of gunfire coming from the town.

Neither horseman was troubled by the noise, for they had both heard a lot of gunplay in their time. They knew that most of the time it meant nothing more than that drunken cowboys were trying to shoot down stars because their cutting ropes were too short.

★   ★   ★

Matt Fallen grabbed his Stetson off the hatstand, looped his gunbelt around his hips and strode out on to the boardwalk outside his office. Fallen tied the leather lace around his sturdy right thigh, checked the seven-inch-barrelled .45, then returned the weapon to its holster.

Front Street was crowded with so many living creatures, both two- and four-legged that it was virtually impossible to see the compacted ground. His eyes narrowed as gunshots rang out around the busy town, but the experienced lawman was unperturbed by the noise. Fallen ran fingers through his dark hair, positioned his hat on his head and studied the street more carefully. Even though shots were ringing out from all four corners of War Smoke nobody in the street much as flinched. Every hitching rail along Front Street was filled with horses tied to every available inch of the weathered poles.

'Listen to them cowpokes whooping it up, Marshal Fallen,' the familiar voice of his deputy called out as he ran towards the tall lawman.

'I hear them, Elmer,' Fallen said in a low drawl as he watched the busy people moving all around the wide street. 'Reckon they're having themselves a good old time.'

Elmer Hook rubbed the back of his neck and came to stand next to the marshal. He appeared slight of build by comparison, even though the deputy was over six feet in height. Fallen had reached just over six feet seven inches before he quit checking. 'I couldn't even get into the Diamond Jug to see my Bessie. The whole place was just full of strangers.'

'Is Bessie the one with the store-bought teeth?' Fallen asked, a wry smile creeping over his square-cut features.

'Them's her own teeth, Marshal,' Elmer huffed. 'Ya shouldn't go saying things like that about Bessie. She'll think I done started a rumour.'

'Sorry, Elmer,' Fallen apologized. His eyes caught sight of two riders who had been forced to draw rein and slow their horses as they entered the end of Front Street. Few men could have spotted the arrival of the two deputies from where Fallen was standing, but then few men were so tall they could see over most other folks' heads.

'What ya seen, Marshal Fallen?' Elmer tried to stretch up to look, but failed to see anything special. 'What ya looking at?'

'Well, Elmer. I'm looking at a couple of shining tin stars heading our way,' Fallen replied. 'And, by the looks of the tall stallion that one of them boys is riding, it's the famed Kid Palomino who's aboard.'

'If'n he's so famed how come I ain't heard tell of him?'

'Trust me. He's a legend.' Fallen gritted his teeth and looked all around at the crowds of people milling in every direction. There were far too many of them and Fallen had already taken three dead men to the undertaker's since most of the strangers had arrived. 'He's the sort of deputy we need around here to help us keep the peace until them herds head north, Elmer.'

Another couple of shots rang out in the distance.

Elmer screwed up his face. 'Ain't heard nobody screaming or the like. I don't reckon anyone was shot.'

'Let's hope them cowpokes don't start tangling with the other drifters who seem to have bin attracted to War Smoke, Elmer.' The tall lawman sighed. 'I got me a feeling in my craw that a hell of a lot of the *hombres* here are nothing better than gun-slingers or worse.'

18

'What's worse than gunslingers, Marshal Fallen?' Elmer asked as the two riders managed to steer their horses closer to the lantern-lit building where they were standing.

'Plain ordinary killers, Elmer, that's what,' Fallen answered. He moved to the edge of the boardwalk. The hitching rail was filled with a line of horses.

Kid Palomino touched the brim of his hat as he and Red stopped their mounts just behind the line of horseflesh. 'Howdy, Marshal.'

'Howdy, boys.' Fallen smiled at both riders and then turned to his loyal deputy. 'Take the boys' horses out back to the yard, Elmer. Water and grain them.'

The Kid and Red dismounted, handed their reins to Elmer, then watched the lean deputy lead both horses up an alley.

'Ya made good time,' Fallen remarked.

'Sheriff Cooper gave us our orders and here we are,' Red replied. He followed the Kid onto the boardwalk.

19

'How is old Coop?' Fallen asked, gesturing for the two dust-caked men to enter his office.

'Still ornery,' the Kid answered.

'And still fat,' Red added as Fallen closed the office door behind them.

'This town sure is busting its stitching and no mistake,' observed Palomino. He rested a hip on the edge of Fallen's desk and removed his gloves. 'Any trouble so far?'

Fallen nodded. 'Yep. Had three strangers killed in drunken fights in the past week alone.'

Red sat down on a cot near the back wall. 'We're here to help ya keep a lid on this stewpot. Right?'

Fallen again nodded. 'Yep. I've heard a lotta good things about you boys, and if anyone can stop this town spilling any more blood, it's you.'

The marshal sat down at his desk. 'It'll be dangerous. Last year I got shot myself, trying to stop two crooked gamblers from burning down the Red Dog.'

Suddenly the sound of a terrified raised voice drew all three men's attention. The Kid was the first to reach the window; he stared out into the amber-lit street.

'What is it, Kid?' Fallen asked, rising quickly to his feet.

Kid Palomino looked at Fallen. 'It's a rider. He looks real shot up, Marshal. He's also wearing a star.'

'What?' Fallen raced across his office, hauled the door almost off its hinges and stared out over the heads of the horses tied to the hitch rail at the rider who was bathed in the light of the porch's lantern.

Red and the Kid peered over the shoulders of the marshal.

'Ya know him, Marshal?' Red asked.

'I sure do. It's Sheriff Race Hawkins.' Fallen gulped as he forcibly pushed his way between the horses at the hitching rail and closed the distance between himself and his old friend.

As the marshal reached the man, who was covered in his own blood, fell into

21

his arms. As gently as was possible Fallen eased the sheriff down to the ground.

'What happened, Race?' Fallen asked.

Hawkins's eyelids fluttered until he was able to see the troubled features of the marshal. 'Matt. Thank God I found ya before . . . '

'Who did this?' Fallen probed.

'Santiago and his band of cutthroats.' Hawkins gasped weakly as he tried to keep conscious for long enough to tell his tale. 'Me and my two deputies was heading here to give ya a helping hand. Then as we was cutting through the pass near Rio Concho we run into them.'

'Santiago Del Rosa?' Fallen said the name as though he had just chewed on a cactus. 'That maniac has crossed the border again?'

'Yep.' Hawkins coughed and a trail of bloody spittle crept from the corner of his mouth. 'Got himself a small army with him as well.'

Fallen glanced around. 'Where's ya

deputies, Race?'

'Dead.' Hawkins tried to rise but failed. 'They was no match for that many rifles and guns, Matt. They was cut down before we even knew what was happening.'

At that moment Doc Weaver forced his way through the crowd and knelt beside Fallen. He too knew the man with the bullet holes in his torso. 'Take it easy, Race. Everything will be OK. Can ya carry him to my office, Matt?'

'Sure enough, Doc. Lead the way.' Matt Fallen stood with the sheriff cradled in his arms and followed the silver-haired doctor along the street towards Weaver's office.

Red Rivers leaned into the Kid. 'What in tarnation is going on, Palomino? What have we ridden into?'

'I ain't sure, but I'm gonna find out,' the Kid answered.

Rivers knew the look in his friend's eyes. 'Hold on. Ya ain't hankering to go looking for trouble, are ya?'

There was a brooding silence. Kid

Palomino stared at the sheriff's horse, which was covered in the dried blood of its master. He took the reins and led the animal towards the dark alley where their own mounts had been taken by Elmer only moments earlier.

'We come here to help Fallen keep the peace, Kid,' Rivers said as he trailed the younger man. 'Not go off half-cocked looking for trouble.'

'I'm riding down to Rio Concho after breakfast, Red,' the Kid announced. 'Ya gonna come with me?'

Rivers sighed. 'Guess so. Reckon someone gotta cover ya damn tail.'

★ ★ ★

Theo Weaver had been a doctor for more years than he could recall. In every one of those years he had never managed to overcome the grief that he always experienced when all his medical expertise failed to save a patient. A huge sigh filled the room as his hands dipped into the bowl of already pink

24

water. He started to scrub the gore from his fingers and hands.

'Damn it all, Matt,' Doc ranted. 'I never can get used to losing my battle with death.'

'Death got all the high cards, Doc,' Fallen said from the easy chair close to the window. 'The thing is, ya beats him sometimes. Most of the time.'

The elderly medical man picked up a bar of soap and dug his nails into its yellow surface. 'Race didn't deserve to die like this. He was a real solid lawman, like you. Most of them bullets I dug out of him was in his back.'

Fallen rose to his feet and stepped closer to the table where the naked Hawkins lay. 'I noticed that. Backshot by a bunch of locobeans led by a maniac who thinks he's a general when in fact he's just insane.'

Doc dried his hands. 'Santiago.'

'Yep.' Fallen rubbed his jaw. 'This has gotta be the third time that killer has ridden north, looking for easy money.'

'Race said he had himself a small

army with him this time, Matt.' Doc tossed the towel away and sat down, staring at the body on his table. 'Why do folks want to be something they ain't?'

Fallen could not take his eyes from the dead man in front of him. He knew that one day another lawman might be staring down at his own remains. 'Why do folks wanna be kings? Reckon it must be the power they crave. Anyway, we'll never know.'

'Ya gotta be a tad loco to understand mad men.' Doc opened the drawer of his desk and pulled out a bottle of whiskey and placed it down in front of him. 'Ya want to join me drowning my self-pity, Matt?'

'I'll have a snort just to be sociable,' Fallen answered, with a nod.

Doc pulled out two dusty glasses and blew the cobwebs out of them. Then he filled them with the amber liquor. 'Here.'

Fallen moved to the doctor and patted his shoulder. 'Don't go beating yaself up, Doc. Nobody could survive being shot that many times. I'm surprised that Race managed to reach War Smoke in that condition.'

Doc downed his whiskey and refilled his glass. 'I reckon I'll have me a few more of these before I crawl into my cot.'

The marshal swallowed his drink, placed the empty glass down on the desk beside his oldest friend, and walked to the door. 'I'll go and wake up the undertaker. Tell him he's got a brand-new customer.'

The first rays of sunshine, heralding a new day, filled the office briefly as Doc Weaver watched Fallen leave his office. The elderly doctor lifted the glass to his lips again. From beneath a wrinkled brow his eyes looked at the body on the long table.

'To you, Race.' He toasted the lifeless sheriff and swallowed the fiery drink. 'My apologies, old friend.'

Fallen opened the door of his office and watched as Elmer woke up and raised his head from his folded arms on the desk blotter.

'Did Palomino and Red manage to find themselves rooms in town, Elmer?' he asked the drowsy deputy.

'Nope.' Elmer got to his feet and walked to the black coffee pot that rested on the top of the stove. 'They lit out just as the sun rose.'

Fallen closed in on his deputy. 'Where'd they go?'

'The Kid said something about them going to Rio Concho.' Elmer rubbed the sleep from his eyes. 'Now why'd they wanna go there, Marshal Fallen?'

The marshal's face went ashen. 'They've gone after Santiago, Elmer.'

2

The bandits surrounded their leader on a high ridge only an hour after they had attacked the lawmen the previous day. Their search for easy prey appeared to have been satisfied. For, like cowardly vermin, these were creatures who preferred their victims to be helpless.

Santiago Del Rosa considered himself a general, as most well-armed men with a small militia always did in a homeland which reeled from one revolution to the next. His chest was covered with tarnished medals: medals that he had no right to wear. Bullet belts crossed his chest atop a red frock uniform of which he had relieved its original owner. Golden tassles hung from each shoulder and an officer's sword rested against his left hip.

He was a man who ranked himself a general, but he had none of the refinements that most genuine officers had. Santiago was merciless. His mission was to pillage the vast territories across the border and return to his homeland with enough riches to make him an emperor.

Yet, for all his finery and arrogance, Santiago was exactly like the rest of his kind. The only difference between himself and those who followed him was that there was nothing he would not do in order for his ambitions to be fulfilled. There was no limit to the depths to which he would stoop to sustain the masquerade.

Santiago Del Rosa could have chosen to attempt his climb to his goal honestly, but that was not his way. He had no desire to try and then fail. He knew that there was a more certain way to reach the heights that others had already attained. You stole a gun and then you became as ruthless as all of your enemies combined. His was a heartless soul. Whatever he wanted he made sure he got. It had taken the twenty-seven-year-old only half a decade to become what he now was.

Feared.

Riding at the head of his band of horsemen, Santiago knew the pickings would be plentiful in this land. The land of the Stetson and the six-shooter. He knew that some men in this country had managed to become wealthier than he could ever imagine possible. Even the poor in this country were rich compared with his countrymen back across the wide river. They had not been forced to catch and eat vermin to survive.

This was America.

It was ripe for the taking, and Santiago intended to take as much as he could get his hands on. Nothing would be sacred to him, for he was on a mission.

Texas had once belonged to Mexico, and as such he considered it his birthright to take anything he wanted from it. Everything these people possessed belonged rightly to Mexico and it was his intention that one day soon Mexico itself would become his.

Santiago's eyes widened as he studied the ranch below them.

There was a ranch, cut out from the woodland which had once dominated this part of Texas. At least 200 longhorn steers filled its fertile pastures, whilst a large ranch house stood at its centre. Barns and other smaller buildings were scattered around the large house, where smoke billowed from a tall stone chimney on the northern wall.

Santiago took a deep breath and then smiled.

'With so many steers I think these people have much for us to take, *amigos*,' he told his followers gleefully. 'I think we shall find much gold down there.'

The most loyal of Santiago's riders were brothers; Luis and Pedro Ruiz. Both drew their horses to either side of the smiling man, who had removed a cigar from a silver case before placing it between his stained teeth.

'Do you think there might be women down there, General?' Luis asked as he struck a match and lit Santiago's cigar. 'White-skinned women taste so much better than those we are used to.'

Santiago nodded as smoke encircled his head beneath the wide brimmed sombrero. '*Sí*, Luis. I think there might be women down there. Women for us to service like the bull.'

'Do you think they are women with golden hair?' Pedro asked excitedly.

Santiago nodded and then spat. 'I think so. There are many golden-haired gringos along this stretch of old Mexico. We shall teach them it does not pay to steal land from us.'

The brothers spoke quickly to the other horsemen who surrounded them, and the sound of thrilled men filled the air.

'But it is the money we want,' Santiago insisted. 'We are here to get as much money as we can and then return back to Mexico. If there happens to be sweet females along the way we shall have our pleasure. It is our right.'

The horsemen all began to chorus in agreement.

'Do you think we should steal the cows?' one of the riders, named Ramon, asked innocently. He was chewing on a plug of tobacco whilst brown drool ran from the corners of his mouth. 'I do not like cows. They are very dangerous.'

'We are not here to steal stinking cows, Ramon, you fool,' Santiago snapped. He pointed his smoking cigar at the house below them. 'We are here for money.'

Luis looked at all the faces around him in turn. 'The gringo money here is worth much more back in Mexico, *amigos*. We shall be as rich as kings when we return with our pockets swollen. Is this not right, General?'

'Exactly, Luis,' Santiago agreed. 'You will all be kings and I shall be your emperor.'

Suddenly they all heard the rustling of movement in the long swaying grass that rose up the hill from the fences set to keep the longhorns secured. Each man drew a weapon and cocked it. Then the swaying grass revealed a small fair-haired boy of about six years of age. Only Santiago resisted the urge to draw his gun as his right hand rested on the hilt of his sword.

The boy paused when he realized that his playground had been invaded by strangers. Then he ventured closer to the large white stallion and looked up at Santiago.

'Howdy,' the boy said.

Santiago knew enough English to return the greeting.

'What ya doing here?' the boy continued.

'We are visitors,' Santiago said. His hand gripped the silver handle of his sword and slid it from its scabbard. The afternoon sun danced off its blade. The boy could not take his eyes off it. It was like watching fireflies dancing.

'Golly. I never seen me a knife that big before,' the child said. His eyes followed the brilliant light which moved along the sword's length. 'Sure wish I had me a knife that big.'

Santiago smiled. 'Tell me. Who is down in the ranch?'

'My ma and sisters,' the boy replied, his eyes following the light of the sun on the blade. 'Pa went to War Smoke with some steers and ain't gonna be back for days. He took all the hands with him.'

Luis leaned from his saddle, towards the child. 'Sisters? How many sisters?'

The boy tried to count on his fingers as he recited their names aloud. 'Daisy, Maggie and Eula. Three.'

'How old are they?' Pedro asked.

'I don't know,' the boy answered. 'Eula and Daisy is full growed, but Maggie ain't. She ain't as old as me.'

'Look.' Pedro stood in his stirrups and pointed eagerly down towards the courtyard, where a female had walked out into the blazing sunshine. 'Look at her hair. It is like the sun itself. Golden.'

'That's Eula,' the boy told him.

'And there are no men down there?' Santiago enquired, touching the sharp blade of his sword with his thumb.

'Nope. All gone with Pa.'

The other restless riders made a guttural sound as they drooled over what they knew would soon be theirs for the taking.

Santiago savoured the smoke which rolled around his mouth and smiled. 'Such hair.'

'They all got yella hair,' the child innocently told them.

'When do we ride down there, General?' Luis asked, his eyes scouting the terrain below them.

Santiago looked at the boy and smiled. 'Do they have many guns down there, little man?'

The boy shook his head thoughtfully. 'Nothing but an old scattergun, but that's on the wall over the mantel. Ain't none of us can reach it without standing on a chair. My pa can reach it, though.'

'Gracious, *amigo*.' Santiago laughed and then, without even the slightest hint of warning, he swung the sword downward. The blade hit the child and continued on through his tiny form. There was no noise from the boy as his blood spewed in all directions from the fatal wound. The child was virtually cut into two parts by the sheer force of the blow. He fell like two sides of a freshly slaughtered pig at the feet of the white horse.

Every one of the bandits stared down at the dead child and then at Santiago, who ran the edge of his sword across his pants leg before sliding its lethal blade back into its scabbard.

'He was very informative.' Santiago grinned before he looped his reins around his left wrist and thrust his spurs backward into the flesh of the white stallion. 'Come, *amigos*. Let us taste the fruits of the golden-haired ones.'

The horsemen spurred.

There was no more chilling a sound

than that of riders with the scent of ripe females in their flared nostrils.

The horsemen travelled quickly down the slope through the high grass, sending dust flying up over their horses' shoulders as they increased their pace. One by one they spurred and then pulled back on their reins as their mounts jumped the fence poles and landed on the level terrain. The startled long-horn steers scattered as Santiago led his men through the lush grassland towards the heart of the ranch.

The young female's face went pale as she stood helpless in the courtyard. She had no idea of what was happening, and she was frozen to the spot. Within a mere heartbeat the riders were dismounting all around her. Luis Ruiz was first to the girl called Eula, and he grabbed her around the waist. His putrid body odour filled her with fear and dread.

Only Santiago remained mounted as he held his mighty horse in check and stared at the long house with its wide-open door. The smell of fresh-cooked food swept over them as the terrified Eula screamed out. A cruel smile came over his features.

Until that very moment the Perkins family had lived a charmed life. They had travelled west from Virginia ten years earlier and had purchased the rundown ranch. Louis Perkins and his wife Anne had spent every waking hour working on it until they had one of the most profitable cattle ranches in southern Texas. In all of that time they had been blessed with good luck. But luck was a two-sided coin and now, for the first time, it fell with its bad side up.

The family had turned the once barren ranchland into an Eden. Everything they required to live a good life could be found on the small fertile strip of cultivated soil.

Now their Eden was to become something else.

Serpents had infested its purity.

'Ma,' Eula shrieked out in alarm. 'Ma!'

In all the days that she had lived in this remote place Anne Perkins had not heard any of her children screaming in the way that Eula was screaming now. She ran from the kitchen out into the blazing sun to witness her eldest daughter being stripped where she stood.

'Eula,' Anne called out, and she began to run towards her.

Luis Ruiz had the struggling Eula under control. He was tearing at her clothing as the rest of the bandits joined in.

Anne Perkins was stopped in her tracks by the powerful stallion which Santiago used expertly to foil her advance.

'Stay where you are, bitch,' Santiago snarled.

'Who are ya?' Anne Perkins yelled up at the bandit.

Santiago looked down upon the handsome female in the way that a man might consider crushing a bug beneath his boot. He tapped his spurs and moved his mount towards her until it was snorting into her face.

'I am General Santiago Del Rosa, bitch.'

'Git them filthy critters off my daughter,' Anne shouted up at the rider. 'And git off my property.'

'Not until we have freed you of your gold,' Santiago replied.

'What? We ain't got no gold,' she shouted.

'Look, lady.' Luis laughed as his fellow outlaws continued their assault upon Eula and her dress was torn to shreds. 'Look at what we are doing.'

'Tell him and them other varmints to quit.' Anne shouted at Santiago.

'Why?' Santiago grinned through the smoke of his cigar at her horrified expression. 'They are men and she is ripe. It is only natural.'

'I'll kill ya,' she threatened.

'I do not think so,' he mocked.

Suddenly her younger daughters Daisy and Maggie emerged from the house behind Anne. They were also

42

calling out in distress at the sight before them.

Anne turned. 'Get back inside.'

Santiago was grinning from ear to ear. He sucked the last smoke from his cigar, then he tossed it aside. He dismounted and walked towards the furious woman. He grabbed her shoulders and lifted her off her small bare feet.

'So many beautiful females,' Santiago said. He leered down at the feisty woman and then dropped her back to the ground. 'So much golden hair. I shall enjoy each of you.'

She backed away and swallowed hard. 'Keep away. My husband and our cowboys will be back soon and they'll kill the whole bunch of ya. Hear me?'

'I hear you.' Santiago raised his eyebrows and stared at the younger girls with equal desire. 'Such a banquet just waiting to be eaten.'

Eula screamed even louder. 'Help me, Ma. Help me.'

Anne stepped closer to the bandit

leader. 'Take me. Do what ya will with me but leave my girls be.'

Santiago pushed her back. 'I will take you all, bitch.'

Anne shook a clenched fist at Santiago. 'My Lou will shoot ya dead unless ya all hightail it.'

The man who thought he was a general grinned.

'But it is such a long way back from War Smoke to here, pretty lady,' Santiago said. 'I think we have plenty of time before he returns to kill us.'

Her face suddenly lost every drop of its colour. She blinked hard and tried to think of how this creature could possibly know where her husband had gone. Then she felt sick as her younger daughters rushed to her side and clung on to her apron strings. There was only one way that Santiago could possibly know where her husband was. It meant that he had encountered her son up on the hillside where the boy played.

Her eyes flashed to the hillside and she knew the truth.

'Ya ain't seen a little boy up yonder have ya?' Her voice was skaking.

Santiago gave out a belly laugh. '*Sí.*'

'He told ya them things?' Anne probed as her daughters clung to her in dread.

'*Sí.*' Santiago loomed over them. The shadow from the brim of his sombrero covered all three females as he reached to the face of the mother and touched her chin. 'We met the little boy. He was very talkative.'

Her heart began to pound as her tear-filled eyes looked up at the high swaying grass, that covered the slope below the trees. She then called out at the top of her lungs. 'Billy? Come here, Billy.'

Santiago began to smile even more widely as a group of his men gathered around them. 'Do not strain that sweet little voice of yours, pretty lady.'

Anne Perkins felt her jaw drop. 'What ya mean?'

'He cannot come to you.' Santiago shrugged as his men laughed loudly. 'He is dead.'

Anne gasped, then a wailing sound came from deep inside her. 'No.'

Her daughters cast fearful glances at each other before they looked to their mother for an explanation.

'What he say, Ma?' Daisy screamed at her mother.

Anne did not reply. Only a wailing sound came from her lips as tears flowed like rainwater from her eyes.

Santiago snapped his fingers. His men swooped from all sides and grabbed hold of Anne and her daughters. The screaming grew louder and more fearful as the four of them were carried inside the house.

Santiago smirked as he followed his men into the dark interior of the ranch house.

By the time he had entered four of the bandits had positioned Anne Perkins on the table and awaited their laughing leader. Santiago walked towards the woman and lifted her dress. His demeanour left no room for doubt as to what he intended to do.

'Make the others ready for me,' Santiago ordered his men as he briefly turned his gaze away from Anne.

The youngsters began to wail in horrified expectation of what was about to happen.

Santiago returned his attention to their mother. 'You should be very grateful, my golden-haired bitch. You shall be the first to be honoured.'

Defiantly Anne spat into his face. 'Ya nothing but an animal. A dirty stinking animal. I ain't afraid of the likes of you.'

With her spittle hanging from his face Santiago carefully positioned himself and then dragged her hips toward him in one violent action.

Anne Perkins wailed out in shock.

'N-no. No,' she cried out.

Santiago ignored her scream.

'Do not thank me, little mother. It is my pleasure.'

3

The blue sky was cloudless. Only three black-winged vultures circled on high thermals, observing the land beneath them as dust rose up off the horses' hoofs and hung in the dry air. The birds soared in wide calculated swoops high above the two horsemen. Whatever it was that the birds had set their eyes upon, it was not the living.

It was the dead.

Even before the riders' noses had alerted them to the kind of horror that lay beyond the sickly-sweet-smelling mist, the buckskin gelding and the tall palomino stallion shied repeatedly as their masters' spurs encouraged them on. Like the birds above the canyon the horses could also sense the rotting of human flesh somewhere ahead of them.

The two riders cut down from the grassy range and entered the canyon. It had been a long ride from War Smoke. The Kid and Red began to slow their mounts as the putrid scent of death filled their nostrils.

'Reckon we found them dead 'uns, Palomino,' Red muttered.

The Kid did not reply.

Palomino and Red had made good time to reach this remote place, known as Rio Concho, so quickly but now they regretted their haste, for they were about to discover that Sheriff Hawkins's words had been true.

The canyon was silent and daunting. It had a story to tell the two horsemen, one that neither of them wished to hear, for it was the story not merely of death but of insane carnage. The smaller gelding led the stallion ever downward until they reached the floor of the canyon.

It was midday and the heat was close to that of an oven. There was nowhere to hide from the blinding rays of the sun, which blazed down upon them.

No shade and no hiding-place.

Yet they knew that they had reached the very place where the deputies and Hawkins had been shot by Santiago and his ruthless cohorts. The golden sand was stained with blood. An awful lot of blood. The two star-packers reined in and stopped their horses inside the mouth of the canyon. The ground was churned up where many riders had ridden across its normally pristine surface. Both riders stared at the sand beneath their feet.

Kid Palomino kept one hand on his leathers and the other gripping the pearl handle of one of his matched .45s. His elegant horse dropped its head and snorted at the sand as the scent of death swept over both riders and mounts.

It was close to noon and the sun was almost directly above the riders as slowly they dismounted.

'This don't make sense, Red,' the Kid said.

'I ain't gonna disagree with ya.' Rivers nodded.

'I seen me slaughterhouses with less blood scattered around than we got here.' The Kid bit his lip. 'So much damn blood. It's all over.'

'Yep,' Red agreed. He pointed up into the misty canyon. 'There was a lotta killing done here, but according to the sand the bodies was dragged away.'

'Why do that?' The Kid sighed, trying to see beyond the mist.

Red Rivers held on to the bridle of his buckskin horse and walked forward, leading the nervous animal behind him. His eyes studied the ground as if it were a book written in some strange tongue and he were its interpreter.

'What's the tracks tell ya, Red?' the Kid asked. He dropped his reins to the ground and paced after his pal.

'Not a lot, Kid,' Red answered. He glanced at his young companion, then returned his gaze to the ground. 'All I know for sure is that them deputies hit the ground here and then were dragged yonder by them bandits. They roped them and then rode up the canyon. If'n them boys was alive when they hit the sand they sure was dead after that, I'll wager.'

The Kid sniffed the air. 'They must be close.'

'Ya right. I sure can smell them too.'

Palomino rested his gloved knuckles on his guns and looked all around them. The sand was dark with dried blood. Blood which seemed to have come from the two deputies.

'Something just ain't right about this, Red boy,' the Kid said. 'There's too much blood to come from just two bodies. What do ya make of all this blood?'

'Easy, Kid. I got me a feeling that them deputies didn't just get shot,' Rivers replied. He straightened up and watched his friend scan the canyon for clues.

'How'd ya mean?' Palomino looked at Rivers.

'Look at the ground,' Red said. 'Folks that get themselves shot fall and bleed. Bleed in one place, unless they drag themselves away, but this ain't what we got here. This blood is everywhere. All over the darn place. There's only one way blood can be spread around like this.'

Palomino came closer to Rivers.

'Spill it out, Red.'

'They was hacked, Kid.' Red Rivers looked at the sand about them. 'I'm thinking Santiago's men hacked them deputies with machetes after they backshot them. Hacked them real bad before them boys fell to the ground. Look at the way the blood fans out all over. That means they was hit by long blades and their blood just flew all over.'

'But where's the bodies?' the Kid pressed.

Red looked at the mist and then at the circling vultures before returning his gaze to his partner. 'I'm betting we'll find what's left of them up yonder.'

Palomino sighed. 'Let's go take us a look-see.'

Red stepped into his stirrup and pulled himself back up on to his horse. 'Yep.'

Kid Palomino mounted the tall stallion and looked at his friend. 'We gotta find them so we can bury them.'

'Smell that stink, Kid. A blind man could find them.' Red tapped his spurs and rode deeper into the canyon.

Palomino followed.

They did not have to go far. The sight which greeted both men as their horses rounded a bend in the canyon wall made even their seasoned guts churn. Neither rider had ever set eyes upon anything quite so horrific before.

This was not what either had expected.

The Kid hauled his reins and turned his skittish mount away from what was left of the two deputies. The smell was sickening as the hot rays of the sun cooked the sand and everything that lay upon it.

Red Rivers had to drive his spurs into the flesh of his buckskin horse to force the nervous creature to walk up to the butchered remains.

The red-bearded rider turned away and stared back at his partner, exhaling loudly. 'Damn it all, Kid. What kinda varmint could do this?'

The bodies had been cut into bits and scattered.

Palomino dismounted, dropped his reins and walked across the sand to what he imagined might be the torso of one of Sheriff Hawkins's men. He stared down. He did not breathe for fear of inhaling even more of the sickening stench rising from the sand. He turned and moved to another more recognizable part of one of the deputies. It was a leg or at least part of one.

The Kid turned his bandanna around and lifted its wipe to cover his face. Flies filled the air all around the body parts, feasting on their unexpected banquet.

'I ain't never seen nothing like this before, Red,' Palomino said. He leaned on Red's saddle and looked up at him.

'Me neither.' Red Rivers looped his leg over his horse's neck and dropped to the ground next to his friend. 'Reckon that bastard Santiago and his scum sure got themselves a kick out of this. Even Apaches would never do nothing like this. There ain't no profit in this kinda thing.'

'This ain't just murder, Red,' Palomino said in a hushed tone. 'This is wholesale slaughter.'

'Them bandits must all be as loco as Santiago.'

The Kid looked over the top of his bandanna at the sight, then pulled his gloves over his knuckles until they were as tight as his skin itself. 'C'mon. We better bury what we can find before them vultures up yonder come down and rip the flesh off what's left of these pitiful critters.'

Red kicked at the sand. 'It's soft enough for us to use our hands, Kid.'

Palomino nodded. 'What about the

tracks, Red? Which way do ya figure Santiago went?'

Rivers knelt down and clawed a hole in the sand at their feet. 'North.'

'Damn it all. There are homesteads and cattle ranches dotted all over north of here, Red.' The Kid knelt and started feverishly to dig another crude grave. 'Them innocent folks ain't got no inkling of what's heading their way.'

'We'd better work fast so we can try and catch them butchers up, Kid,' Red said. He started to work more frantically.

'How many of them do ya think there are, Red?' Palomino asked without looking at his friend.

Red's eyes glanced at the Kid. 'Might be too many. Thirty or maybe even forty by the amount of tracks yonder.'

Kid Palomino did not respond. He kept working at dragging sand from the hole he had created. A hole he knew he was going to have to fill with the parts of two fellow star-packers.

Their hard labour took nearly half an

hour. With the sides of their boots the sweat-soaked deputies dragged the last of the sand over the two crude graves; then they paused. With trembling hands Red pulled out his tobacco pouch and started to sprinkle fine tobacco dust on to a paper.

'We ain't never faced this many *hombres* before, Red,' the Kid remarked. 'We might be biting off more than we can chew.'

'Won't be the first time,' Red said.

Palomino nodded. 'Hope it ain't the last.'

'I ain't troubled none. We got an edge on them. We ain't loco. That ought to help.' Red ran his tongue along the gummed edge of his cigarette paper and his thumb and fingers rolled the cigarette.

The Kid watched his friend strike a match and draw on its flame before he blew smoke at the crude graves. 'I figure we can slow them up a tad, Red. Pick a few of them off before they gets the better of us.'

Smoke from the cigarette hung in the hot canyon air. Red nodded and walked back to his horse. 'Yep. We can whittle them down a tad. We might even kill the whole sorry bunch of 'em.'

'Ya reckon?' Palomino smiled.

'Hell no.' Red grinned, letting smoke filter between the remnants of his teeth. 'I was just trying to encourage ya a little.'

Palomino jumped, poked his boot into his stirrup and swung his right leg over his saddle. 'Enough gabbing. C'mon. They got themselves a real big start on us.'

Red held on to his saddle horn and eased himself on top of the buckskin. He gathered his reins in, then felt the hairs on the nape of his neck rise. He looked straight at the Kid and was about to speak when a long black shadow from above them on the canyon wall crept between their horses. Both men stared at it for a while.

'We got company,' Red said through a cloud of smoke.

'Keep that hogleg holstered, Red.' Palomino squinted up at the figure, who had his back to the sun.

'What is it?' Red whispered. 'Is it one of Santiago's varmints?'

'I ain't rightly sure,' the Kid replied. His eyes kept staring at the silhouette. 'The sun's behind him. He's on a small pony by my reckoning.'

Red tossed the cigarette away, looked down at the shadow on the ground and studied it hard. He gulped and gave a loud sigh.

'Hell. If I ain't mistaken that's an Injun shadow, Kid. I can make out his fancy hair poking up like a porcupine's quills.'

The Kid looked at the long shadow between their two horses and nodded in agreement. 'Ya right. Sure don't look like no Mexican bandit.'

Red eased his head around and cast his gaze up to the ridge. 'How long do ya figure he bin up there watching us, Kid?'

'Long enough to have killed us if'n he'd wanted.'

'Yeah,' the older rider agreed.

Kid Palomino somehow smiled. 'If that don't beat all. Bin one of them kinda days, ain't it, Red? For all we know there might be a whole damn war party hiding up there waiting to ride down and scalp us.'

Red slowly turned his mount and raised a hand to try and shield his eyes from the glare of the sun. 'I'll tell ya something, Kid.'

'What?' The younger horseman kept a firm grip on the reins as his powerful horse pawed at the sand with a hoof. 'What can ya tell me, old friend?'

Red pushed his hat on to the back of his head and folded his arms. 'I can tell ya that it ain't an Apache up there. He's an Injun but he sure ain't no Apache, Kid.'

Palomino leaned across to his pal. 'And just how can ya tell that, Red? The sun's on his back and we can't make out nothing about him coz we're looking straight into the sun. So how in tarnation can ya be so damn certain that critter up there ain't an Apache?'

Red looked at him and smirked.

'We're still alive. That's how.'

Palomino raised an eyebrow. 'What?'

'An Apache would have killed us before we even seen his shadow, Kid. They don't hanker to white folks.' Red returned his eyes to where the strange figure watched, and his bearded jaw dropped. 'Nope. Whatever that critter is he sure ain't no Apache and that's a fact. And that fancy spiked hair sure ain't from these parts either.'

'It ain't?'

'Nope. That critter is from the Dakotas or even further north of there.' Red unwrapped his reins from around the saddle horn and held them with his left hand as he eased the quarter horse around. 'And I'll tell ya another thing as well.'

Kid Palomino shook his head. 'I'm listening.'

'He's gone.'

Kid Palomino looked back up at the canyon rim and felt his throat tighten.

The Indian was gone as silently as he had arrived. He slapped the shoulder of his companion.

'C'mon, Red. Let's ride.'

Both horses thundered back along the canyon to where the fertile range began. They spurred hard and followed the route taken by Santiago and his band of cut-throats. They knew that the bandits had many hours' lead on them. Many hours in which the merciless Santiago and his followers might kill even more helpless victims.

The Kid and Red stood in their stirrups, whipped the rein tails and urged their mounts to find even more pace. It was a race against time and both deputies knew that the trouble with time was that it had a way of being cruel.

Real cruel.

4

War Smoke was filling with even more people as the afternoon drew on. It was as though every drifter within a hundred square miles had been lured to the sun-baked town by the annual start of the trail drives. But as the seasoned marshal had already realized when he had sent for additional deputies to help him, most of those who were now filling its streets had nothing at all to do with driving steers to the northern railheads. These were men who knew that there were easy pickings to be made when so many people gathered in such cramped and crowded places.

Matt Fallen had not seen quite so many men dressed in elegant clothing for over a year. The best and worst cardsharps and professional gamblers knew that War Smoke was a town where a man could make his fortune if he worked it right. Pickpockets had also been drawn into the sprawling settlement by the knowledge that opportunities like this were rare and not to be wasted.

Apart from Kid Palomino and Red Rivers there had been no other lawmen arriving in War Smoke since the dying Sheriff Hawkins had somehow made it to town. Fallen knew that unless the Kid and Red returned unscathed he would be in exactly the same position as in previous years: alone, with only Elmer to assist him.

So far since sunup the town had been quiet. Fallen walked along his daily route and entered Front Street. The crowded street and boardwalks made the tall lawman pause. It was hot and he was thirsty.

He pushed the swing doors of the Diamond Jug apart and entered the saloon. Even when filled to capacity there was always a gap at the bar for the marshal. Fallen closed up to the wooden counter and a beer suddenly appeared before him.

'Marshal.' Fred Wall, the barkeep, nodded as the rest of the saloon's patrons kept quiet and watched the tall man with the tin star pinned to his chest.

'Thanks, Fred. It sure is hot out there.' Fallen poked finger and thumb into his vest pocket and placed a coin on the counter. He downed the cold beer and nodded. 'Same again.'

Wall lifted the empty glass as suds rolled down inside its glass belly. 'Ain't heard no shooting for a few hours.'

Fallen surveyed the faces watching him. 'It's still mighty early, Fred.'

⋆   ⋆   ⋆

The hot afternoon sun blazed down over War Smoke as a contented deputy sat outside the marshal's office watching the world go by. Elmer Hook had a way of sitting which was almost an art form, especially when he had spent far too long sipping whiskey in the Red Dog. The sleepy-eyed deputy rested a

66

boot against the porch upright and rocked the hardback chair, which he regularly polished with his britches, to and fro on its back legs. Elmer would only quit rocking when he either miscalculated and fell on to his rump or was distracted by a pretty face.

Doc Weaver's was not a pretty face but it sure had a lot of seasons carved into it. The doc ambled at his usual pace along the boardwalk until he reached the sleepy deputy. He dragged another of the weathered chairs from beneath the window and placed his weary bones upon it.

'Elmer,' Doc said, pulling out his pipe from his coat pocket and tapping it on the arm of the chair. 'I see ya well liquored-up again, boy. Why'd ya smell like bread?'

Elmer stopped rocking and looked over his shoulder. 'Howdy, Doc. Ain't it the nicest of days? Sunny and all. What was ya saying about bread?'

'I said ya smell like bread.' The medical man smiled as he sucked on the stem of his pipe. He noticed flour on the sleeves and shoulders of the deputy. 'Bin courting again, Elmer?'

Elmer blushed and vainly tried to sit upright beside the doctor.

'No, I ain't bin courtin', Doc. I bin sparkin' a little with Lucy though.'

'Lucy from the bakery?' Doc grinned as his left hand found his tobacco pouch and opened its leather flaps. 'That explains the flour.'

'Yeah.' Elmer sighed heavily. 'She's awful pretty. Kisses up a storm. So darn friendly. I ain't never met no one so friendly like Lucy is.'

'Awful friendly gal,' Doc said. He forced tobacco into his pipe's bowl with an expert index finger.

The deputy looked with half-closed eyes at Doc. 'That's right enough, Doc. Lucy sure is mighty friendly. How'd ya happen to know that?'

The doc's old eyes stared at the thronging street filled with wagons, horses and people. Keeping those eyes diverted from the younger man, Doc gripped the pipe stem in his teeth and returned the pouch to his coat pocket. 'When I say friendly I don't mean she goes around saying 'Howdy' to folks, Elmer. I mean that she's awful friendly. Maybe a little too friendly for her own good, if, ya gets my drift.'

Elmer rested a bony elbow on the arm of his chair and his face screwed up. 'I don't rightly know what ya mean, Doc. Friendly is friendly, ain't it?'

'In a way.' Doc struck a match, brought it to his pipe and sucked for a few seconds. Smoke billowed around the old man's derby hat. 'But some gals can be a little too friendly with too many young bucks.'

Elmer jolted upright on the chair. His befuddled brain somehow grasped what his older companion was trying to say. He waved a finger. 'Just hold on a cotton-picking minute there. Lucy ain't that kinda gal, Doc.'

Doc tossed the match away and stared through his bushy eyebrows at the deputy.

'Listen up. I'm the doctor in War Smoke, Elmer. Right?'

Elmer rubbed his hands over his face. 'Well, everybody knows that, Doc. What's that got to do with the price of belly pork?'

'The only doctor in War Smoke,' Doc added, tapping his fingertips together over his watch chain. 'Folks come to me when they need remedies to cure all sorts of ailments. Right?'

Elmer nodded. 'Right enough.'

Doc pushed his hornrimmed glasses up his nose and looked straight at the deputy. 'My professional oath don't allow me to talk to anyone about other folks' problems but I can say that everybody comes to me when there's something wrong. Everyone including young friendly gals who work in the bakery.'

'Lucy bin to see ya?' Elmer gasped. 'She ain't poorly is she, Doc? What's wrong with her?' Elmer leaned even closer to his wiser, older friend.

'I can't say.'

'Is it bad?' Elmer gulped.

'Not truly bad but it sure itches her a whole lot.' Doc grinned.

Elmer sat back and pondered the crowded street. 'I wondered why she was scratching like an old hound trying to get rid of an ornery flea, Doc. Ain't catching is it?' Elmer dropped his voice to a whisper.

Again Doc shrugged.

Elmer sighed heavily. 'Ya can't catch it through kissing though, huh?'

'Where was ya kissing her, Elmer?'

'In the yard out back of the bakery,' Elmer told him.

'Take the advice of an old man, Elmer. Stick with Bessie,' Doc suggested. 'Apart from them store-bought teeth she's a mighty fit young gal.'

Elmer was about to protest when he caught sight of Marshal Fallen come out of the Diamond Jug and start to make his way across the busy street towards them. 'Oh deary me. I done forgot to make Marshal Fallen's coffee. He'll skin me alive.'

Doc held on to the arms of his chair as Elmer scrambled to his feet and bolted into the office. He then concentrated on the wide-shouldered Fallen and puffed out a chain of smoke signals that only the marshal could read.

Fallen had barely reached halfway across the busy street when he heard a disturbance in the Golden Garter gaming house. Voices were raised and a few people ran out into the already crowded street. The marshal turned on his heel and headed back to the gambling house. He stopped beside a hitching rail as a young cowboy jumped down from the boardwalk and bumped into him.

The lawman grabbed the cowboy's collar, hauled him up off his feet until he was dangling under his nose and then shouted at him.

'What's going on in there, boy?'

The cowboy looked and sounded scared. His shaking words seemed to stick to his teeth in their attempt to escape his mouth. 'T-t-trouble.'

Matt Fallen shook him even harder. 'Quit babbling, son. Spit it out.'

'Some of the players at the faro table reckon the dealer palmed some cards, Marshal,' the frightened cowboy answered before he was released.

'There's gonna be bloodshed in there, Matt,' one of the local men shouted as he rushed out into the sunlight. 'Black Boone has bin caught cheating and he sure don't like being accused.'

'Boone.' Fallen almost spat the name out as he turned towards the well appointed building, which was set halfway along Front Street. 'That varmint ain't nothing but — '

There was no time to finish his sentence. A deafening shot rang out from the guts of the building and was soon followed by two more. People around Fallen scattered.

'That cardsharp ain't nothing but trouble,' Fallen growled as the crowd between himself and the gaming hall scattered. Fallen quickly stepped up from the street and marched through the open doors of the gaming hall. He could smell the gun-smoke lingering on the stale air.

The marshal stopped and stared down at the body of a cowboy at his feet. An expertly placed bullet hole in his chest was oozing gore. Fallen looked up and glared the length of the long room down to the far wall, where a solitary figure stood behind the faro table with a smoking .44 in his hand.

A dark-haired figure stood admiring his own marksmanship without a hint of remorse before nodding to the marshal. Black John Boone was an elegant man cut from the same cloth as most river-boat gamblers. He wore nothing but black, even including his frilled shirt. He blew down the barrel of his weapon and pushed it under his coat into a hidden holster on his left hip.

'Boone,' Fallen bellowed angrily. The marshal clenched his fists and strode past crouching figures towards the seemingly unconcerned gambler.

'Marshal,' Boone answered with a smile and an air of arrogance.

'You killed another one, Boone,' Fallen snarled furiously as he reached the table. Slowly one by one the gaming hall's patrons rose up to their full height all around the gaming hall. 'How many is that now?'

'Eight,' Black Boone answered quickly.

'Eight? And how long have ya bin in War Smoke?' Fallen pressed, his knuckles resting on the green baize.

'Sixteen days.' Boone sat down, picked up his cigar from a glass ashtray and placed it between his teeth. He blew a line of smoke at the cards set down on the table between them. 'He started shooting before I did. Ask anyone.'

'One dead varmint every other day.' Fallen shook his head and glued his stare to the seated man. Most men would have been afraid but there was no hint of fear in Black Boone. 'A mighty big tally and an awful lotta killing, Boone. I'll bet ya really proud of killing so many innocent folks.'

'It was self-defence, Marshal Fallen,' Boone insisted, gesturing to those who were brave enough to gather around him once more. 'Ask them. That man opened up on me first.'

Fallen looked at the men around the faro table. 'What happened here?'

Jonah Willis, the town mayor, stepped forward. 'The cowboy had lost all his bets and then said Black Boone was cheating, Marshal.'

'He was cussing and threatening Black Boone,' another man added. 'He went down the room and dragged his gun out and started shooting wild. He let two shots go before Boone here returned fire.'

'Boone drew and only fired once,' Willis continued.

Fallen looked to where the dead body of the cowboy lay, and then back to Boone. 'That gotta be close to sixty feet. A pretty good shot for a man being fired at.'

The seated faro dealer smiled and pulled the cigar from his teeth. 'One shot and the trouble ended, Marshal. I could not allow him to fire again. An innocent person might have been hurt or, even worse, killed.'

'That was mighty thoughtful of you, Boone.'

Boone took a mock bow. 'My pleasure.'

'One day you'll make a mistake, Boone,' Fallen warned him.

The smile of the faro dealer grew wider. 'I surely doubt that, Marshal.'

Fallen narrowed his eyes. 'Wanna make a bet on that?'

Black Boone stopped smiling. 'Do I hear the hint of a threat in your voice, Marshal?'

'Unlike the eight men you've gunned down, Boone,' Fallen said in a low whisper, 'I know how to use my gun and I'm never too drunk to hit what I aim at. Do I make myself perfectly clear, Mr Gambler?'

'Like crystal.' Boone nodded.

Matt Fallen turned away from the faro table and retraced his steps to the wide-open doors and the dead cowboy. He looked at the crowd and pointed to a group of the silent men. 'You pick him up and take him to the funeral parlour. Now.'

Four of the men instantly obeyed. Fallen brooded on the pool of crimson at his feet, then glanced over his shoulder at the gambler who had already restarted his game of faro. A cowboy somewhere close to his own age stepped towards the marshal. He looked saddle-weary and more shocked than any of the others inside the Golden Garter. He moved unsteadily towards Fallen as though in total shock.

'Ya any idea who that cowpoke was, stranger?' Fallen asked.

The man rubbed his dirty face along his equally dirty sleeve. 'I sure do, Marshal. I worked for him.'

'He have a name?'

'His name's Lou Perkins,' the stunned cowboy replied. 'He got a ranch just north of the Rio Concho.'

The name of Rio Concho drew Fallen closer to the cowboy. He leaned over the shorter man and whispered in the cowboy's ear. 'Did ya say his spread is just north of the Rio Concho?'

The cowboy nodded.

'Yep. He brung me and another hand named Seth to War Smoke.'

'Why?' Fallen asked quietly.

The cowboy kept looking at the pool of blood. 'We was only in town to sell some longhorns for the cattle drive. I sure don't know who'll tell Annie.'

'Annie?' Marshal Fallen repeated the name. 'Is that his wife, pard?'

'Yep. His wife.' The seasoned cowboy was distraught. 'He got himself a fine lady and four kids back on the ranch. Me and Seth worked for them for five years or more. I gotta find Seth and ask him what we should do.'

The lawman led the cowboy out into the street with his hand on the man's shoulder. The nervous cowboy stopped and looked at the marshal's square jawed face.

'Sweet Lord. Someone gotta tell them about this.' His chest heaved in panic. 'How'd ya tell a good woman and her litter that the man of the family ain't ever coming home again, Marshal? I ain't never had to do nothing like that before. I don't know if'n I can.'

Matt Fallen gave a long sigh.

'Don't go fretting none, pard. That's my job. I'll go and tell them.'

The cowboy stood on the boardwalk and watched as the marshal stepped down to the dusty street and silently negotiated his way through the press of vehicles and people until he reached the other side of the wide thoroughfare. The stunned cowboy then rushed away like a chicken that had just had its head severed.

5

The sky was rippled with a crimson glow that resembled the bowels of Hell in all its fiery horror. The devilish hue lit up the thirty or more bandits as they spurred their bloodied horses up towards a tree-covered hilltop. The vast fertile range opened up and spread from horizon to horizon in front of the line of bandits as their leader eventually drew rein and halted his white stallion in the shade of a large tree. The swaying grass seemed to become lusher the further north they rode after leaving the Perkins's cattle ranch far behind them.

Now the scent of fresh prey filled Santiago Del Rosa's eager nostrils.

The bandit who thought he was an emperor still had the horrific evidence of death upon him. The blood of his latest victims was smeared down his britches where he had wiped the blade of his deadly sword. Yet, like all insane killers, he had already dismissed his most recent atrocities from his mind, for there was new game ahead of him.

New equally innocent game.

His brutal eyes burned through the fading light at the unfenced land before them. This was indeed cattle country and ahead of them another few hundred steers grazed on its sweet grass. Santiago rested his hands on his ornate saddle horn and inhaled deeply.

'Look, *amigos*. This land is crying out for an emperor.' The ruthless bandit spoke loudly enough for all of his men to hear his words. 'We belong here. It is our birthright.'

The other horsemen grunted in agreement.

'I see a ranch, General.' Luis Ruiz pointed towards a bend in a river, where a scattering of buildings could be seen. 'Do you think we shall find more gringo money there?'

Santiago gave a thoughtful nod. '*Sí*, Luis. I can smell their gold from here, but you are wrong to say it is a ranch. I think it is a small town.'

Every man in his ruthless army looked to where their leader was gesturing with his left hand. 'Towns are much better for us. There is always more money in towns. Their banks are like fat little pigs waiting to be stuck. We shall strip that town clean, like the locust strips the crops from the fields. What is theirs shall be ours. This I vow, amigos.'

The bandits gave out a weary cheer.

The dim-witted Ramon ran a hand along the neck of his horse and then shook the foaming flecks of sweat to the ground. 'I think our horses are spent, General. We need to rest them.'

Santiago dismounted swiftly. He looked at the mounts of his men and nodded in agreement. 'Little Ramon is right. Our horses need water and grain before we carry on. It is a long way back to Mexico and we cannot be certain that we shall find good enough horses if we do not look after these. We shall make camp here and wait until dawn before we strike out at that succulent town.'

'Like the rattlesnake,' one of the men whooped.

'Like a whole nest of rattlesnakes,' Santiago joked.

The men dropped to the ground and began to remove their saddles from the backs of their exhausted horses. Steam rose up into the late-afternoon air.

One of the bandits strung a cutting rope through each of the horses' bridles and secured both ends to trees. He then began to wipe the tired horses down.

Santiago's eyes were burning as they kept peering down at the distant town, whilst above them stars started to emerge across the heavens. This was a town which was less than a hours' ride from the place they were readying for camp, but Santiago knew that the first light of sunup was soon enough to strike. Men with sleep in their eyes were far easier to kill than those who had been awake for an entire day. He chewed on a cigar and struck a match across the grip of one of his holstered pistols. He lifted the match and studied its flame. There was not even the hint of a breeze. The flame burned true.

'We shall find much money down there, *amigos*,' he said through a cloud of smoke. 'And many more ripe bitches to do our bidding.'

Pedro had already started to make a camp-fire as his brother emptied one of his saddlebags of its contents on the ground next to his kneeling sibling. Luis looked up at their leader and showed the rich variety of food he had stolen from the ranch, now far behind them.

'Look, General. We have much food to fill our bellies this night. With full bellies we shall sleep the sleep of the angels, I think.'

Santiago smiled and then laughed. 'Indeed. Just like those golden haired bitches we left back at the rancho, Luis. They are sleeping the sleep of the angels.'

As though they had only one collective mind between the lot of them, each of the bandits started to laugh at exactly the same moment as their leader. The sound of their guttural amusement filled the air as the bandit on his knees cupped the flame of a match and ignited the kindling.

'What if the townspeople see our fire, General?' Pedro asked the confident bandit leader.

'They are soft people who live their lives thinking that their god will protect them, Pedro,' Santiago said. He did not take his eyes from the town as signs of lanterns being lit began slowly to show. 'They will not see our fire and even if they do they will take no notice.'

Again the bandits all laughed.

'How much shall we cook, General?' Luis asked, studying the horde of food before him.

Santiago drew his sword and raised it high above his head until the dying rays of the sun caught its length. His cruel eyes were transfixed upon its blood-stained blade. 'Cook it all, *amigos*. There is plenty more where that came from. We shall eat like kings tonight and for the rest of our days. From this moment on we shall never again be hungry. From this moment on we shall have everything we desire.'

A resounding cheer went up.

For one faltering moment all of the bandits believed every single word their leader had uttered. For that brief moment of time, which would be gone as quickly as the setting sun, Santiago actually knew what it felt like to be a real emperor.

He liked the feeling.

6

The Golden Garter was in full swing. The coming of darkness only seemed to draw more men through its doors: men who thought they were going to become rich on the turn of a card or the roll of dice. Yet none had ever managed to beat the odds which were so cleverly stacked against them. The gambler clad entirely in black walked out into the eerie amber light of countless lanterns. He paused to cup the flame of a match in his soft, skilful hands and inhale the smoke of his expensive cigar.

'When are ya going to do it, Black Boone?' the mayor asked him as Jonah Willis emerged from the shadows and stood beside the cardsharp. 'Ya bin here for weeks and ya ain't made a play for doing what I paid you to do.'

Boone turned and looked into the

face of the sweating man. He smiled slowly as smoke traced through his teeth. 'When I'm good and ready, Willis.'

'I paid ya two hundred dollars to come here and kill him,' Willis added.

'A mere deposit, Mr Mayor,' Boone said, and began to walk along the still busy boardwalk towards his hotel.

Willis grabbed the gambler's sleeve and halted his progress. 'What? Ya takes two hundred dollars from me and say it's just a deposit?'

'You don't think you can hire my services for a mere two hundred dollars do you, Willis?' Boone pulled his arm free and continued onwards down the street as the throng of men and women brushed past them. 'I want another eight hundred and then I'll kill him, clean and sweet.'

'Eight hundred bucks?' Willis croaked in shock. 'Where am I meant to lay my hands on that kinda dough?'

Again Boone paused. 'The same place that you stole the first two hundred from, Mr Mayor. The town's accounts, which I know you oversee because you are so trustworthy.'

Willis thought for a moment, then nodded. 'OK. I'll get ya damn money but ya gotta do this soon. That damn Fallen has ruined my plans for years. He's too damn honest and I've had me enough of that kinda law being pushed down my throat. OK. I'll get ya damn extra money.'

'When?' Boone sucked in smoke and then blew it up at the stars.

Suddenly their attention was drawn to the funeral parlour across the street. Four men carried a coffin out of the brightly lit building and slid it on to the back of a buckboard. One of the men then returned to the funeral parlour. Two of the others mounted saddle horses whilst the tallest of the group climbed up on to the driver's seat of the vehicle and released its brake.

Willis and Boone eased back into the shadows as the buckboard and its outriders passed them.

'That was Fallen,' Willis said.

'I know that, Mr Mayor,' Black Boone said, tapping ash from his cigar. 'Where do you figure he's going?'

Willis looked Boone in the eyes. 'That cowpoke ya killed earlier. He must be taking him back to his ranch.'

'How long will he be gone?'

'Two days at most,' Willis replied. He followed Boone along the boardwalk until they reached the hotel. The gambler placed a hand upon its brass doorhandle. 'Tell me, when are ya gonna kill him? How long have I gotta wait, Boone?'

'I want the rest of my money tomorrow. Agreed?'

'I'll have it in ya hands by ten in the morning, Boone,' Willis promised. 'Now tell me. When are ya gonna kill him? I gotta know so I can be out of town. When will ya kill that righteous Matt Fallen?'

Black Boone opened the door and stepped into the well-appointed lobby of the hotel. He smiled. 'Two days at most.'

7

It was dark and only the eerie light of a half-moon and countless stars illuminated the vast country in front of the two horsemen. Yet the trail had not been too hard to follow for the wily red-haired rider who led his younger companion across the range of high, sweet grass. When thirty or more heavily laden horses rode across even the hardest of terrain they left their mark. When driven across soft fertile ground covered in grass they left a scar that even the blindest of people could follow.

Red Rivers rode ahead of his partner, hanging over the side of his saddle and squinting hard at the disturbed ground every inch of the way. His well-trained quarter horse required no instructions to keep it moving. This was nothing new to the sturdy mount. Both horses gradually ascended the steep rise until they reached the high tree-covered ridge which overlooked the Perkins property. As the buckskin gelding reached the very top of the rise it snorted and then shied.

It took every ounce of the rider's prowess to keep his mount from bolting.

'Easy, boy,' Red said as he fought with the restive horse beneath him. 'Easy.'

'What's wrong, Red?' Palomino asked, steering his own mount up behind the nervous quarter horse. He eased back on his rein. 'He ain't seen a sidewinder has he?'

'Ain't no snake could make this nag buck like this, Kid,' the older rider replied after he had managed to steady his horse.

Palomino leaned over his saddle horn. 'Something sure spooked him. Any idea what?'

Silently Red looped his reins around his saddle horn, then dismounted slowly into the tall grass. He held his bridle for a few moments, kicked at the grass, then turned round to face the Kid. 'Holy Moses.'

'What is it, Red?' Quickly Palomino looped his leg over the head of his mount and slid to the ground. He moved to the side of his partner and looked innocently to where Red was staring.

Palomino gasped.

'Just like them deputies,' Red said. He turned away from the horrendous sight and walked towards their mounts. 'Cut up like he was just meat on a butcher's slab.'

Kid Palomino knelt. 'Hell. He's just a little 'un, Red. No more than five. Why would Santiago do this to a defenceless little kid? Why?'

'That's easy. He done it coz he can, Palomino,' Red answered. He rested against the side of his tired horse. 'Some critters just got a sickness in their heads. They keep doing stuff like this until someone stops them.'

'Reckon it's up to me to stop him.' Palomino rose angrily to his full height. He was visibly shocked and sickened. He paced around and exhaled loudly before noticing the shingle rooftops of the buildings below them, now bathed in moonlight. It looked a tranquil scene but they both knew that more horrors probably awaited discovery. 'Look down yonder. A ranch.'

'Yep. A ranch where we're gonna find more dead 'uns.' Red gathered his reins, poked a toe into his stirrup and pulled himself on to the back of the buckskin.

The Kid grabbed his saddle horn, swung up on to his horse and turned the tall animal around. 'Ain't no lights on down there.'

Red nodded. 'That's what troubles me, Kid. If there was anyone alive down there they'd have at least one light burning.'

Palomino looked at his pal. 'Ya figure the rest of this family met with the same fate as the boy, Red?'

Red pointed at the grass which led down the slope towards the fence poles. 'Yep. The grass bin stomped down mighty hard by a whole pack of horses, Kid. Them bandits went to that ranch house and I got me a gut feeling the killing didn't stop with that young 'un. When vermin get the taste of blood in their mouths they kinda keep killing. Their kind never can quite satisfy their hunger for killing.'

The younger deputy allowed his powerful palomino to rise and kick at the night air before he tapped his spurs to alert the animal that their quest was not over yet.

'C'mon, Red.' Palomino steered his stallion down the steep grassy slope. The mighty horse leapt over the fence poles easily and then thundered across the courtyard towards the ranch house. The quarter horse followed suit. Both horsemen rode on until they had reached the place where the ground had been churned up by dozens of horses hours earlier. Even the eerie light of the half-moon could not hide the fact that many horsemen had ploughed up this ground long before these two had arrived to investigate.

Palomino held his reins up to his chest and looked all around them. It was as silent as the grave and both riders knew why. The older man looked straight ahead of them at the house. Its door was wide open. Its interior was in darkness.

The air was quite cold, but neither horsemen noticed.

Palomino jumped to the ground, dropped his reins, moved to the side wall of the house and plucked a lantern off a rusty nail. His fingers fumbled for a match.

Swiftly Red dismounted, walked past his friend and carried on alone through the door.

He struck a match, then blew it out again instantly.

The Kid had reached the doorframe when his partner's hand pressed against chest and stopped him in his tracks.

Both men looked into each other's souls for a few seconds.

'Why'd ya blow the match out, Red?' Palomino asked, raising the lantern in his gloved hand.

'Ya don't wanna see what I just seen, Kid,' Red said in a voice that was shaking in a way that the younger man had never heard before.

Palomino stared at his friend. 'Let me pass.'

Both of Red's hands were on the kid's chest, forcing him back to where their horses were standing. 'No, Palomino. Ya don't wanna see that. I sure wish I'd not seen it.'

The Kid stopped trying to pass Red and dropped the lantern.

'What's in there that could be worse than we seen up on the hill, Red?'

'Ya wouldn't believe me even if'n I told ya,' Red gasped as if his guts had been kicked by a mule. 'I seen me a lot of bad things in my time but I never set eyes on nothing like I just laid eyes on.'

Kid Palomino had no stomach for

seeing whatever it was that had upset his partner so badly, but there was no other way. Not in his book. You never shied away from the truth however bad that truth was. He placed his hands on the older man's shoulders and moved him aside. Palomino walked into the darkness, then stopped. For a few endless moments his eyes could make nothing out but then, as they slowly adjusted to the shafts of moonlight which flooded through the open windows the Kid at last began to see.

He felt his entire body shake. He wanted to run but knew that he could never outrun the vision of depravity that would now be branded into his memory for the rest of his time.

Not even his wildest nightmares could have prepared him for the sight which greeted his young eyes. It was far worse than the horrific things he and Red had seen during the preceding hours back at the Rio Concho canyon and up on the hill.

His fingers groped for a match in his

jacket pocket but then he thought better of casting even more light upon the bloody outrage. This was not the sort of barbaric sight which required illuminating any further. Not, anyway, if a man wanted to be able to close his eyes again and sleep.

His knees had turned to jelly. The Kid wanted to sit down but it was impossible. Nothing inside the ranch house had escaped the splattering of gore from the blade or blades which had done this.

He looked down at his boots and could make out things which chilled his soul. The deputy wanted to throw up, but knew that there were enough bodily fluids left here without him adding to them. Kid Palomino carefully turned and retraced his steps out into the fresh air. For a few moments the young man just stood and slowly inhaled crisp night air until he felt his innards settle.

The only thing which had not greeted both men when they entered the house was the stench of death. That meant the pitiful females had been killed when the sun was already setting and the day had start to cool. They had not had time to start to decay just yet. That last indignity would come with sunrise.

Red was sitting on a tree stump. The uncanny light of moon and stars could not hide the young deputy's ashen pallor from the older man's wise eyes.

'I told ya not to go in there, Palomino,' Red said with a sigh.

'I know ya did, old pal.' The Kid rested a hand on his friend's shoulder and patted it. 'I thank you for that, but there are times when a man has to see things with his own eyes before he can figure them out.'

Red watched as Palomino began to walk slowly across the courtyard towards the high-walled barn. 'Where ya going?'

Palomino did not turn but spoke anyway.

'Gonna try and find us a couple of shovels.'

Red pulled out his tobacco pouch.

'Good thinking, boy. At least we can bury what's left of them before sunup.'

Suddenly a familiar sound caught the older deputy's attention. It sounded like a dozen hornets cutting a trail through the air.

Red stood still as an arrow hit the ground in front of him. His wrinkled eyes watched as the arrow vibrated for a few seconds, then he looked up in a vain attempt to see the archer.

Palomino returned with two well-used shovels over his shoulder when he noticed the arrow a few feet from Red's boot toes. He lowered the shovels, rested them against a tree stump and pulled the arrow free of the ground.

'I didn't notice this before, Red.'

Red swallowed hard and snatched the arrow from his friend's hands. 'That's coz it weren't there before, Kid.'

Palomino's eyebrows rose. 'Ya mean it just got here?'

'Yep.' Red kept searching for the elusive Indian whom they had briefly encountered back at Rio Concho. 'Our

Injun pal is back.'

'What's the arrow tell ya?' the Kid urged.

'I figure he wants a powwow,' Red answered, keeping his gaze on the arrow.

'Are you sure?' Palomino questioned.

Red nodded. 'He's had two chances to kill us and he ain't taken them, boy. This fella wants to talk.'

The confused younger man ran a gloved hand over his mouth. 'Why would an Injun wanna talk with us? That don't make no sense, does it?'

'Depends on what he has to say or tell us, Kid.' Red placed the arrow down on the tree stump and plucked up one of the shovels. 'Let's dig some graves and fret about him later.'

Silently Palomino picked up the other shovel and trailed Red to where there was a patch of softer ground. As his boot pushed the shovel into the earth so many questions filled his mind.

Who was the unknown shadow archer?

Why was he making his presence known to them?

Why had he not killed them when he had the chance?

Was Red right? Did he simply want to talk?

So many questions and not one single answer.

They kept digging.

★ ★ ★

It had taken the better part of three hours to bury the bodies and the sky was starting to lighten. Stars slowly faded as the blackness of night became a strange, haunted hue. This was the time that most people never witnessed, the time when night turned to day. The two deputies sat exhausted on the ground that they had just patted down with their shovels and stared out across the cattle-covered pastures. Neither knew whom they had just laid to rest, but that did not matter to them. They had done what all good men do and provided the dead with a little dignity.

Somewhat more than ten minutes after they had finished their back breaking work the sound of movement caught Red's attention, causing him to hit his partner's leg with a fist.

'Hear that, Palomino?' Red asked, feeling the hairs on the nape of his neck start to rise again.

The Kid nodded. 'I heard it a few minutes back when you was snoring, Red.'

'Must be that Injun,' Red surmised. He turned slightly and tried to see.

'It is,' Palomino agreed.

'How'd ya know for certain?' Red asked.

Kid returned his partner's leg punch and pointed with a gloved finger. 'Look.'

Red looked in the direction that Palomino was indicating. Through the morning half-light a shimmering image was approaching on a painted pony.

'Make him out?' the Kid asked.

Red gulped. 'Yep. I was right. He's a Dakota Sioux.'

'Never heard of them.'

'That's coz most of them is dead.' Red swallowed hard.

'He ain't.'

'If we ain't careful, we will be,' Red warned. 'Them critters ain't got a happy bone in their whole bodies. One false move and he'll put arrows between our eyes before we can clear our holsters.'

Kid Palomino sighed and pushed his hat off his brow. 'Great. You've really cheered me up a whole heap there, Red. For a moment I thought we were in trouble.'

8

The two exhausted deputies sat and stared into the morning haze as the sun prepared to rise before them. An uneasy glimmer of trepidation rippled through their veins as the morning light slowly began to defeat the darkness. Both the men with tin stars pinned to their vests had grown used to the darkness, as though it had offered them a shield against unseen danger. Now what their eyes focused upon filled them both with nothing but dread.

Just as Red had proclaimed, this was no ordinary Indian who rode towards them. This man was nothing like the Apaches they were used to encountering in this untamed land along the border. Both the tired lawmen knew this man astride the painted pony was totally out of place here.

He was from another place.

Another world.

This was no near-naked Apache they were watching as he fearlessly steered his mount towards them. This Indian was far leaner and taller than the half-starved Apaches who frequented both sides of the unmarked border. He looked virtually regal in his highly coloured finery. There was nobility in his well-defined features. Strength and courage were chiselled into the emotionless mask of his face. A face set beneath a strange hairstyle of trimmed bluebird feathers woven into his shining black hair. Black plaits of hair decorated with silver rings hung to either side of his dark-skinned face.

His clothing was pale fringed buckskin decorated with patches of coloured beaded pictures. There was no doubt in either deputy's mind that this was a true warrior who could probably kill them both in a mere heartbeat should he so choose.

He held a small bow across his lap, over the neck of the pony, whilst a quiver filled with arrows rested against his hip. Both bow and arrows were black.

The warrior stopped his pony and stared down at the seated deputies with unblinking eyes, as though he were unsure what course of action to take.

Should he kill them or talk?

All three men knew that it was his choice to make.

Not a sound came from the magnificent warrior as he held his pony in check while his long legs dangled lower than his mount's belly. He was studying them intently. Whatever he was thinking would remain secreted inside his brain.

Both the tired lawmen knew that seated on the ground was possibly the worst place they could have chosen to be when faced by someone who was obviously capable of killing them. Yet the warrior did not show any sign of wanting to harm them. Was this mere curiosity, both deputies silently asked themselves?

'Now I'm kinda scared, Red,' Palomino admitted, resting his hands on his outstretched knees. 'Who is this critter and what does he want with us, Red?'

'That's a damn good question, Kid,' Red whispered. 'This man sure ain't what I thought we'd run into in these parts.'

'Is he a Dakota Sioux like ya figured?'

'Yep.' Red nodded.

'Can ya speak his lingo? Palomino asked, wondering whether he should try to stand or remain seated. Focusing his eyes on the arrow resting on the bow string Palomino decided it was far safer to remain seated.

Red Rivers bit his lower lip. Long before he had met the man now sitting beside him he had spent many years in what was then known simply as Indian territory. Since that time Red had not even set eyes upon any of the various Plains tribes, let alone tried to communicate with one of them.

'It's bin more than twenty years since

I last bumped into one of these Dakotas, Kid,' Red said drily. 'I ain't sure if I can recall his tongue. None of them northern tribes speak the same language.'

Kid Palomino smiled at the warrior. 'Howdy.'

There was no sign of a reaction in the face of the rider. He just kept staring down at them as though he were trying to work out what they were.

'He's definitely a Dakota, Kid,' Red said again. 'I ain't seen one of them since I was younger than you are.'

Palomino looked at his partner. 'Hold on a minute, Red. If none of them tribes can talk to one another how do they manage? They have to meet folks from other tribes, so how do they talk?'

Red scratched his beard thoughtfully.

'And more to the point, how are we gonna have us a powwow with him?' Palomino added before Red could reply.

The Indian suddenly moved and

pointed at Palomino.

'Powwow.' The warrior repeated the familiar word and gave a jerking nod of his head. 'Powwow.'

'He knew that word, anyways,' the Kid said.

'Damn it all. I was right.' Red blinked hard. 'For some damn reason he does wanna talk to us. But why?'

Palomino ran his sleeve across his sweating brow as daylight grew brighter around them. 'Do you know any other words besides powwow, Red?'

'To be honest, not too many,' Red admitted. 'I done forgot most of the different dialects I once used when I traded with them different tribes.'

'Powwow,' the Indian said again, this time more loudly.

Red eased his backside across the soil towards his friend, then turned until his mouth was close to the Kid's left ear. 'I remember one thing though, boy. Them tribes up north speak to one another using sign language. All of the tribes use the same hand signals to talk to other tribes.'

'Are ya sure?'

Red nodded. 'Damn right. Watch this.'

Kid Palomino watched as Red used his hands to speak to the watching rider. Then, to the younger man's surprise, the Dakota began to return hand gestures.

'What ya both saying?' Palomino asked Red.

'Hush up,' Red snapped from the corner of his mouth, whilst his hands continued to talk. 'This ain't easy. I ain't done it for the longest while.'

Palomino waited until both Red and the Dakota stopped using hand signals for a few moments before he spoke again.

'Well?'

'I was right. He is a Dakota. Maybe the last of them, by what he was telling me.' Red sighed sadly. 'Damn it all. There used to be thousands of them in the Black Hills. Mind you, that was before the white men found out about all of the silver and gold in them hills.'

'What's he doing here?'

'Same as us,' Red answered as he and the Dakota kept talking to one another with their hands. 'He's following them bloodthirsty bandits. And Santiago.'

'Why?' Palomino watched nervously as the warrior dismounted and stood looking at them.

Red Rivers shook his head. He then began to tell his partner what the warrior had just told him.

'He tells me that the last of his people fled down to Mexico a few years back to escape the cavalry's retribution after the Little Big Horn. Anyways, there was only about fifty of them left. Mostly old folks and kids. Only three warriors remained after the trouble north. They lived in peaceful isolation until Santiago and his men raided their camp.'

Palomino rubbed his jaw. 'Ya don't have to go into detail about what

Santiago and his cronies did to them.'

Red nodded. 'Yep. Exactly the same as they done here.'

Kid Palomino looked up at the stern-faced warrior. The more he looked the more he could see the pain carved into his features.

'How'd he survive, Red?' Palomino wondered. 'How'd he manage to escape being massacred along with the rest of them?'

'He was off hunting. He couldn't get back in time to help his people. They were all killed. Slaughtered like they was nothing better than vermin. He did say that he saw the man in charge of the bandits, though. Their chief, as he calls him. A crazy man on a white stallion wearing a fancy outfit and wielding a sword.'

'Santiago,' Palomino said angrily through gritted teeth.

'Yep.'

'What's he want with us, Red?'

'He wants to join us to trail them bandits and then be allowed to kill

Santiago,' Red replied.

The younger deputy nodded as he and his friend managed to get to their feet. 'That's fine with me, pard. We need all the help we can muster.'

The warrior was taller than both deputies. He stepped closer, pointed at their tin stars, then gave a nod. His hands spoke to Red and the older lawman smiled.

'What he say?' Palomino asked.

'He said he knew that we weren't like the animals who killed his people coz we was wearing tin stars,' Red replied. Just then the sun emerged from over the horizon and the ranch suddenly became bathed in light. 'Ya might not know it but these tin stars saved our lives, Palomino.'

'Ya mean that if we hadn't bin sporting these stars he'd have killed us, Red?' the Kid asked.

Red raised a bushy eyebrow. 'Reckon so. He's bin hunting riders who killed his people. Without these stars we'd have just looked like two more riders and that's what he's bin hunting. Riders.'

Kid Palomino sighed and then swallowed hard. 'He got himself a name, Red?'

The older deputy's hands asked the question and then his wrinkled eyes read the reply.

'Black Wing.'

9

Black smoke billowed up into the morning sky from what remained of the town called Sweet Water. It curled and twisted heavenwards like a dark serpent's tail and wings. Flames were spread across the entire town from what remained of the wooden buildings. Bodies littered the empty streets. They were the bodies of innocent, peaceful people who had been taken by surprise by the gang of rampaging bandits as they swept across the range from their temporary camp a few moments after dawn. Dead horses and dogs also lay on the bloody sand of the now deserted streets of Sweet Water. The females had lasted a little longer than their menfolk, but that had been no mercy to any of them. For what all of them had experienced in the aftermath of the brutal destruction was little better than a massacre. Every female had been defiled with equal inhumanity and once used they had been mercilessly dispatched.

Blackened timbers were all that remained of the numerous buildings which, only hours before had made up the entire town. The bank had fared a little better than all of the other buildings in Sweet Water, but once its safe had been opened it too was torched and razed to the ground.

It had all happened in the blink of an eye, or as swiftly as the opening of a cactus flower when the sun spreads across the land as sunrise comes at last. These were men who knew only one thing: to kill, and they did it well. Nothing seemed to have survived their guns amid the choking smoke which rose from so many smouldering foundations. Nothing but the memories of those who now lay dead after their settlement had been overrun by the filth from south of the border.

Once again mere bullets had not

been enough to quench the bloody thirst of their insane leader. Once more he had butchered the dead and dying with his long sword before leading his small army of reprobates on to new victims.

Santiago Del Rosa now had the riches of an entire town filling the saddle-bags of his followers: a fortune in gold capable of making his corrupt dreams appear a little more plausible. Yet Santiago and his men had not turned their horses and started back to their homeland with the spoils of their actions.

Even though they now had more than enough money and gold to allow them to live as kings across the border, Santiago had decided to continue onwards. He had the taste of blood and the sound of screaming females in his heartless soul now. He was like the gambler who could never quite win enough to satisfy his insatiable avarice.

Their hoof-dust lingered in the still air as the sun rose higher and hotter.

Even a few hours after the thirty or more bandits had ridden away following their sword-waving general the dust from their horses' hoofs remained suspended a man's height above the ground. It hung like the ghosts of those whom the bandits had abused and then slain. The choking black smoke from the charred timbers of what had once been buildings continued to swirl up into the cloudless blue sky.

Laden down with the spoils of his brutal attack, Santiago Del Rosa had then made his first mistake since leading his men into Texas. He had assumed that if they continued forging a route northward the grass would become even sweeter and the pickings grow ever richer.

It was an error made before by many others unfamiliar with this part of the Lone Star state. Texas was unlike many other territories; there were many variations of terrain and climate. It had been said that a rider could travel through every known climate in the space of twenty-four hours. Snowcapped mountains and blistering deserts lay side by side. Only altitude separated their equally deadly terrains for the unprepared.

Being totally ignorant of the land they had chosen to invade the venomous Santiago and his mindless followers forged ahead ever further north. If what they had encountered so far was anything to go by they believed that greater treasures awaited them in towns filled with even more fair-haired females.

Leading a score of heavily laden packhorses in their wake the bandits drove on. The trail north of Sweet Water gave no clues to the unwary of what lay ahead. Steep trails led up a forested hillside which in turn led to a place of which only those who had knowledge of this land knew anything. If Santiago had led his small army in any other direction than due north, he would have found what he sought: lush land filled with wealthy towns and prosperous cattle ranches.

As the line of horsemen rode on in single file, leading their packhorses in tow up the narrow trail, they had no inkling that they were heading for one of the most infamous places in southern Texas.

10

If anyone looked the epitome of respectability it was the mayor of War Smoke. Yet as ever it was not wise to judge the contents of a book by studying its cover. Jonah Willis was a man who had never been quite what he appeared to be and although he had been elected to office three times he remained what he had always been. He was a corrupt mystery and very, very rich. Few had any idea of the source of Willis's wealth before he arrived in War Smoke. If he had his way they never would discover the truth. For like all men who dealt from the bottom of the deck with an ease that he had mastered years before, Willis always kept the cards pressed against his silk-vested chest.

Like a pestilence he contaminated everyone and everything he touched.

He shared in the profits of nearly all of the town's brothels and saloons as well as two of the town's many gambling halls, but even they were not enough to satisfy his insatiable greed.

Willis always desired to build his corrupt business into something resembling an empire to equal those he had read about back East. It seemed to him that all of his plans to achieve this goal had been blocked. Blocked by the one man in War Smoke whom he had never been able to taint with his own tarnished brush.

Marshal Matt Fallen had stopped Willis building new whorehouses and kept his boot on the neck of all of the mayor's other dubious business endeavours.

For more than five years Willis's fortunes had been held in check by the one man in War Smoke who could not be bribed. Matt Fallen had used the rule of law to maintain his control of an otherwise lawless settlement. For men like Willis there could be too much law;

too many restrictions choked what he thought of as opportunities.

Jonah Willis wanted the old ways to return, when the West was truly wild and men did what they damn well liked and used gunlaw to fend off any who tried to prevent them.

The marshal had little idea of how much hatred Willis had for him, but soon the honest lawman would find out.

The morning sun blazed along Front Street as Jonah Willis reached his office set at the end of the long thoroughfare. The mayor had just withdrawn $800 in cash from his bank. He had only just placed his hat on his desk and pulled his swollen wallet from his coat pocket when the door opened again behind him.

Willis swung around and stared at Black Boone as the gambler entered and moved towards him.

Willis gasped at the silent figure who sat on the corner of his large desk. 'Black Boone!'

126

The gambler touched the brim of his black hat. 'Willis.'

'Ya scared the damn life out of me,' Willis said, mopping his brow with a lace handkerchief.

'It grieves me to think that I came so close and yet failed to put ya six feet under.' Boone smiled and eyed the fat wallet in the mayor's hands. 'I've bin waiting for you but you're late in paying me my money.'

'Patience is a virtue.'

Boone stared hard at the sweating man. 'When I give a time for an appointment I stick by it. I demand the same of others.'

Willis cleared his throat. 'I'm the mayor. I don't have to answer to you.'

'You're also a yella belly who wants a real man killed, Willis.' Boone snatched the wallet from the greasy hands, unfolded its leather and smiled at the contents. He pulled the wad of bills from it and began to count. 'Just remember that if you ever try to cross me I'll kill you as well.'

'Mighty big talk, Boone. Just when will ya kill Fallen? When are ya gonna do it?' the mayor pressed the man, who folded the sixteen bills and pushed them deep into his pants pocket. 'I have to know. I've deals to arrange. Mighty big deals.'

Boone tossed the empty wallet back at the mayor, stood up and adjusted his shirtsleeves so that his cufflinks were visible.

'I've decided to hasten his demise, Mr Mayor.' Boone said bluntly in a low tone.

'What?' Jonah Willis was unsure of what his hired killer had said. 'Speak English.'

'I'm gonna kill him sooner than I planned,' Boone glossed.

Willis looked excited. 'When? How? Ya know that Fallen left town?'

Boone smiled. 'I shall ride out from town in an hour and follow the trail left by Matt Fallen,' he told Willis. He walked back to the office door and stared out into the bustling street. 'I shall kill him out on the range.'

'I thought ya was gonna do it here?' Willis panted.

'I've changed my mind.' Boone tapped the brim of his hat and opened the door wide. 'Out on the range there will be no witnesses. Witnesses can be a tiresome problem.'

'Problem?'

'Indeed.' Boone grinned and patted his pocket where he could feel the wad of banknotes pressing at his thigh. 'I would hate to have to kill lots of problems as well as Fallen.'

'But how will I know that ya done the job and earned that money I paid ya, Boone?' Willis asked.

'If I am successful I shall return.' Boone replied with a shrug.

Willis moved towards the gambler. 'But what if he kills ya instead? How am I gonna know if the buzzards pick ya bones clean out on that damn range?'

Black Boone grinned. 'Don't fret, Mr Mayor. I'm the fastest, most accurate shot in the West. Matt Fallen is a marked man and soon you'll be dancing on his grave.'

Jonah Willis watched as the door closed and the man in black evaporated into the crowd.

He swallowed hard and then began to tremble.

Suddenly, for some reason that he could not comprehend, he was afraid. Very afraid.

★   ★   ★

It was getting hotter on the vast range between Rio Concho and War Smoke. Matt Fallen had not stopped forcing the buckboard's team of horses on towards his goal during the hours of darkness. He would have pressed on if it were not for the fact that the two cowboys had drawn rein to rest and water their mounts. Only then had the marshal brought the buckboard to a rest. The sun had risen a few hours earlier but neither the lawman nor his outriders had apparently noticed. There was still a long way to go before they reached the remote ranch and delivered the coffin, but Fallen had something else on his mind. Something more engrossing than staring at the tails of horses for another hour or so. From his high perch on the driver's board he had noticed the black smoke rising up into the sky off to his left, and he was curious.

Fallen dropped down to the ground and hauled the large feed and water bags off the flatbed, where they had been loaded beside the coffin, and carried them to where the horses snorted. He proceeded to feed and water the animals. Then he rested his knuckles on his gunbelt and returned his attention to the smoke.

Cowboys Seth Riley and Pete Hope had both worked for the Perkins family long enough to have grown to think of them as the families neither of them had ever had. The pair were watering their lathered-up horses when they noticed the tall marshal pull the brim of his hat down to shield his eyes. Fallen stared out to where the land fell away from the high range, the spot where the smoke climbed into the sky.

Riley was first to speak to the lawman. 'What ya seen, Marshal?'

Fallen pointed. 'Do ya see that smoke, friend? My eyes are kinda dust-filled and I ain't too sure if I'm seeing what I think I'm seeing.'

Both cowboys turned to see where the tall marshal was staring. Both cowboys noticed the black smoke which trailed up into the blue heavens.

'I see it.' Hope spat a lump of brown goo at the ground.

'Yeah, I see it as well. What do ya figure that is burning over there, Marshal?' Riley asked.

Never taking his eyes from the black smoke as it curled up into the sky, Fallen marched to the two cowboys.

'Which direction is the Perkins ranch, boys?' Fallen asked them anxiously.

Riley pointed southward. 'Thataway.

The smoke is miles away from Lou's place.'

Hope nodded and spat again. 'That's right. The only thing over there is Sweet Water.'

'Sweet Water.' Fallen rubbed at his jawline. He could feel the fresh growth of whiskers which had grown during the long drive to this spot. 'Anything else out that way? Any ranches or smallholdings?'

Both men shook their heads.

'Just the town,' Hope said. 'The ranchers tend to live high there. They all have fancy houses in the town rather than roughing it out on the range with their livestock.'

'What ya thinking about, Marshal?' Riley asked looking up at Fallon's concerned face. 'Something sure seems to be gnawing at ya craw.'

Fallen shook his head. 'That sure is an awful lot of smoke coming up from over there. The amount of smoke you'd figure would come from something big burning.'

'Reckon so,' Hope agreed.

'Something big burning, like a building, ya mean, Marshal Fallen?' Riley asked.

'Yep. Or maybe a whole bunch of buildings burning.' Fallen rubbed his neck as he considered the body in the coffin on the back of the buckboard and the obvious fire. He was torn between continuing on to the ranch with the cowboys or satisfying his curiosity and finding out what was making so much smoke.

'Is it part of ya job to go looking into things like that?' Hope asked the lawman.

Fallen looked at both men. 'Yep. It sure is. That's what I'm paid to do, boys. Be doggone nosy and keep the peace. That's why I'm wearing this marshal's star. I should be heading over there to find out about that fire.'

'But ya can't be in two places at once, Marshal,' Riley observed.

'Seth's right.' Hope spat. 'No critter, no matter how clever he is, can be in two places at the same time.'

Suddenly Fallen thought about Sheriff Hawkins and how the dying lawman had told him that Santiago had crossed the border with his army of ruthless killers. A cold chill clawed at Fallen's spine.

'Santiago,' Matt Fallen said through gritted teeth.

'What ya say, Marshal?' Riley asked.

Hope spat again. 'He said Santiago.'

'What the hell is one of them?'

'As long as the marshal knows what it is . . . ' Hope nodded.

Fallen pulled his gloves from his gunbelt and slid them over his large hands. He flexed his fingers and looked at the smaller of the cowboys.

'Feed and water ya horse fast, friend,' Fallen told Hope.

'What for?'

The marshal patted the cowboy's shoulder.

'I'm borrowing it for a while,' Fallen said.

11

With shaking hands Mayor Jonah Willis unsteadily poured another glass of whiskey into the large tumbler set on the blotter before him. He downed the drink as he had done with the previous half-bottle, then stared sadly at the quarter-inch of amber liquor that remained. He lifted the neck of the bottle to his lips and allowed the strong whiskey to burn a route over his tongue and down his throat. The bottle was finished and, in a strange way, Willis felt as though he too were as redundant as the empty vessel.

No amount of whiskey had been able to relieve the lingering doubts which crawled over his skin like maggots. He wanted to forget what he had done but he could not. He wanted to try and quell the fear that ripped into him, but again he failed.

His bleary eyes glanced to the wall clock which seemed to be getting louder as its second hand methodically clicked around the clock face. Then he cast his attention to the street, which he could see from his desk chair over the green half-blinds hanging from a brass pole. A line of saddle-weary cowboys rode down the centre of the street to where the vast herds of longhorn steers grazed. Front Street was still crowded and still noisy and yet all Willis could hear was his own heart inside his overweight shell.

With the door secured he ought to have felt safe inside his office but he did not. It was impossible to lock out something which was inside you. He could feel the tendrils of fear wrapping around his every sinew. No wolf could have terrified him to his very guts as mercilessly as his fear of the arrogant gambler done since Black John Boone had left the office some time earlier.

Black Boone had said he would be starting out on his mission in an hour,

Willis recalled. Had Boone actually said that? Or was the whiskey filling his mind with even more inaccurate recollections? The mayor feverishly rubbed his face but felt nothing. The whiskey had numbed him to everything except the fearful trepidation which continued to torment him.

Why was he afraid? The question lingered without resolve.

He had hired the best man with a six-shooter that he had ever seen, yet Willis was still petrified. Willis knew only too well that Matt Fallen was not an easy man to kill and the mayor had seen many try and fail to achieve that seemingly simple task.

He toyed with the empty bottle, then stood up.

Willis tottered to the window and rested his hands on the brass rail which supported the lower blinds. He teetered as his head spun trying to cope with the half-bottle of whiskey he had consumed since Boone had departed.

An hour. He was sure that Boone had

said he was leaving in an hour. Had it been a hour? It had been long enough for him to finish the bottle of hard liquor off.

Willis steadied himself, screwed up his baggy eyes and stared out into the street. It was like looking at an ocean of bodies passing in every direction, but he tried to concentrate on the side street which was opposite him. He knew that the town's main livery stable was up that narrow track and most men leaving War Smoke used it after they had retrieved their horses.

The mayor felt sick as the hard liquor washed around inside his empty stomach, but he knew he had to keep watching. He had to see the gambler riding out with his own eyes.

For what felt like an eternity Willis clung on to the brass rail and forced his drunken eyes to keep watching. Then he saw him riding slowly down towards Front Street.

'Boone,' Willis whispered to himself.

Even in trail gear Black Boone cut a

dashing figure. Even seated astride a horse the gambler looked every inch the Southern gentleman.

The gambler eased back on his reins and looked over the heads of the crowd at the sweating figure in the window. The man who had hired him to kill Marshal Fallen.

Jonah Willis was open-mouthed as his sore eyes stared at the horseman who teased his mount into the main street of the sprawling town and touched the brim of his hat to everyone he passed.

The gambler crossed the street on the gleaming horse which, like its master, looked every inch the thorough-bred. Boone paused for the slightest heartbeat outside the mayor's office, glanced straight at his paymaster and grinned.

Willis gave a pitiful nod and the rider was gone.

Gone to do what he had been hired to do.

Gone to kill Matt Fallen.

Or try.

The mayor turned so that his back was to the window and tried to calm himself down. His heart raced. It had started and there was no going back. He had set the ball rolling and there was no way on this earth that he could now stop it. The dominoes had already started to fall and they would keep falling until the last of them lay flat down on its face.

Just like one of those men who would encounter one another out on the range far beyond War Smoke. Either Fallen or Boone would never return.

What if Black Boone failed?

Willis felt the beads of sweat trickle down his jowls. What if he told Fallen who it was that had hired him and then failed to kill the marshal?

What then?

What would Fallen do?

If Matt Fallen survived he might return to kill the gambler's paymaster. A torrent of dread washed over the mayor.

Unsteadily, Willis grabbed his hat,

placed it on his head and fumbled with the door key until the door opened. He stepped out on to the boardwalk and somehow managed to insert the key back in the lock. It clicked; he dragged it clear and pocketed it.

He needed more drink.

Enough drink to make him forget. Willis staggered through the crowd of men, women and children towards the sound of the nearest tinny piano and the scent of stale tobacco.

Yet with each faltering step the mayor knew that there was not enough hard liquor in all of War Smoke to make him forget what he had done.

He reached the swing doors of the Red Dog and pushed his way into the saloon. His feet shuffled through the sawdust towards the far wall, where he could hear the sound of glasses and bottles as well as smell the scent of whiskey. Everything he looked at was blurred and yet the doubts inside his brain were still crystal clear. He reached the bar counter and slammed a dollar on to the wet surface. A bottle of the cheapest whiskey in town was pushed towards him. He pulled its cork and lifted the bottle to his lips. He drank long and hard.

When he lowered the bottle a chill raced the length of his spine. He looked at his blurred reflection in the mirror behind a stack of glasses.

'What have I done?' he mumbled.

12

The ground beneath the hoofs of the bandits' horses was brittle and crumbled as the line of riders ascended the perilous trail up the mountainside. Santiago Del Rosa had realized an hour earlier that he had made a grave mistake in leading his men up the steep mountain trail in search of fresh prey. But, like all men who consider themselves leaders, Santiago would never admit his error. Halfway up the densely forested mountainside the powerful white stallion had begun to encounter trouble as it negotiated the winding narrow route, fit for only goats. Yet Santiago would not let his powerful mount stop its ascent. He mercilessly whipped and spurred the big creature ever upward towards the summit. Far too late the bandit leader had realized that it was impossible for any of them safely to turn their horses around and return down to the flat range which was now far below them. They had to persevere and keep heading towards the high pass set between the two tree-covered peaks. There was no alternative but to forge on regardless.

Like the general he pretended to be, Santiago kept bellowing his words of encouragement. It was an irrational exercise, for those who followed could do little else but keep heading upwards.

Ragged brush cut through Santiago's uniform into his flesh as the maniacal horsemen battled with the sharp thorns that seemed to cover every vine and overhanging tree-branch. There was only one choice open to him, his men and the packhorses they had commandeered, and that was to carry on.

The moans and groans of those who trailed their leader grew more and more intense the higher they were forced to ascend. Santiago vigorously hacked at the overhanging tree branches with his bloodstained sword yet even his mind-less resolve was beginning to falter. He wondered whether this torment would ever come to an end.

The long line of drunken horsemen kept spurring their horses to go on climbing the trail behind the white horse. Each of the bandits knew that their quest for even more juicy pickings had led them unguardedly into a place where none of them wanted to be.

Only the tempting sight of the pass set between the tree-covered twin-peaked mountaintop gave them any hope that soon their travails might end and they would again find a terrain they were more accustomed to.

Higher and higher they travelled as both the sun and the temperature rose remorselessly. The atmosphere beneath the cover of the trees was stifling. If these men had been sober at the start of this perilous trail maybe none of them would have followed Santiago. But none of them had been sober after they had razed Sweet Water to the ground. It had taken a lot of hard liquor to wash away the memories each of the depraved riders had accumulated inside their maddened brains.

The plentiful supply of whiskey that they had looted from Sweet Water gave them solace that soon their plight would end. The trail was littered with the empty bottles dropped by the horsemen as they kept heading up towards the seductive summit to which Santiago was leading them. A bellyful of rotgut whiskey made it easier to tolerate the thorns of a million razor-sharp brambles. It also made it easier to blot out the awareness of danger that sober men might be capable of fearing.

'We are almost there, *amigos*,' Santiago called out to ears which either did not understand or simply did not care. 'Keep going. Soon we shall find even more beautiful women for us to bless with our seed.'

The bandits followed. There was no option. They kept whipping and spurring their mounts. The pitiful animals kept obeying, kept managing to climb the steep trail. The mountain pass was now within spitting distance and the bandits thought that soon their discomfort would be nothing more than a vague memory. Yet none of the drunken bandits had any notion that over the mountain, through the pass, lay another land. A totally different land from anything any of them had ever encountered before. A land that would make the steep climb they were now enduring seem like paradise.

More empty bottles were discarded. The men were excited. They could see the pass clearly now through the trees. So close. So very close. The hard liquor was strong enough to numb their senses long enough for them to see Santiago reach the pass and wave his sword triumphantly above his head.

'Come, *amigos*. Now we shall ride down into the valley and teach the stinking gringos another lesson,' he cried out. 'I have brought you to the land of milk and honey. Let us drink our fill of the spoils of this land.'

One by one the bandits reached the only level ground on the entire mountain. They lined up behind their leader and saw the fire in his eyes as he hacked at the low tree-branches to reveal the start of the trail which would lead them down the opposite side of the mountain.

Even with blood running from their torn flesh none of the bandits felt anything except relief that they had at last reached their goal. They cheered their leader as Santiago allowed his stallion to rear up and stroke the air with its hoofs.

'Did I not tell you that we would conquer this stinking little ant hill, amigos?' Santiago shouted out to his exhausted followers. 'Come.'

They erupted in cheers once again.

After steadying his mount Santiago drove his spurs into the flesh of the white stallion again and steered the weary animal through a wall of overhanging branches and down a descent. The trail was rocky on this side of the pass and the sound of the horses' hoofs rang out. Like obedient sheep the bandits trailed Santiago down into the dimness of the tree-covered slope. They already knew that they were richer than any of them could have imagined possible, yet Santiago promised them even more.

The trail beneath them was wider than the one they had laboured to climb up and it seemed different. Very different. It was not set beneath a forest of trees but was formed on a ledge out from a wall of rock. For a while no one in the line of riders could see anything but the dense vegetation that flanked them as they navigated their way down the treacherous trail.

The further they descended the more the bandits could see shafts of burning sunlight cutting through the canopy of trees ahead of them. The temperature continued to rise, but none of the bandits had any idea why.

Soon they would discover exactly why.

Soon the ruthless bandits would realize they were being drawn down into the bowels of Hell itself.

A place called Satan's Claw.

13

The shimmering air before the three horsemen blackened as a flock of vultures with bloody flesh hanging from their hooked beaks lifted off the ground. The dust-caked eyes of the riders watched the massive birds as they flew up into the safety of the cloudless sky. Kid Palomino, Red Rivers and Black Wing had reached the outskirts of the smouldering debris which until dawn had been known as Sweet Water.

The rising sun had not been kind to the dead, who had been hacked to bits wherever thay had fallen in the now burned-out town. The stench of decomposition filled their nostrils but it was the now familiar sight of the brutal carnage which chilled them the most.

They stopped their mounts as they reached the creek. The animals dropped their heads and started to drink from the fast-flowing water as their masters studied the devastation before them. Palomino and Red stared at the red sand and then cast their attention to the silent Dakota warrior beside them. Black Wing's hooded eyes looked away, for they had seen this atrocity many times before.

Only the blackened ground and scattering of dead bodies gave any hint to what had existed along-side the fast-flowing creek only hours earlier. The choking smoke still rose up into the heavens from timbers which refused to quit burning. For a moment the riders considered crossing the unmarked boundary, but then realized that there was no point.

There was nothing any of them could do except bury the bits of human remains that the vultures had not already stolen. But there was no time for such humane niceties. Only time to try and catch up with the animals who had done this and prevent them from doing it again.

Kid Palomino stood in his stirrups and tried to calculate how many people had been murdered but it was impossible. He looked at his partner.

'It would take until sundown to bury all these folks, Red.'

Red gave a nod. 'We gotta catch Santiago and his dogs before they strike again, boy.'

Black Wing eased his pony away from the deputies' mounts and looked down at the trail which led north. His eyes did not miss anything. The warrior looked back at Red and began to use his sign language frantically.

'What's he trying to tell ya, Red?' Palomino asked as he stroked the neck of his drinking stallion.

Red looked to his friend. 'He's all fired up. He reckons them bandits have headed up the mountain yonder.'

Kid Palomino looked at the mountain a mile north of the burned-out town. It was a daunting sight.

'Hell! They went up there?' The Kid exclaimed. 'They sure don't make it easy to follow them, do they?'

Red swung round and chuckled. 'Don't ya get it, Kid? They've taken the mountain trail. The damn idiots have taken the mountain trail.'

'So?' Palomino looked puzzled. 'All I know is that we're gonna be sitting ducks if we try and follow them up there. One rifleman could hold off an army from up there. How are we gonna catch them now?'

Black Wing watched both his companions silently. He knew why the older deputy looked so amused.

'That trail leads to only one place, and that's a fact,' Red said gleefully. 'Ain't no turning back once ya starts up it. Old Santiago don't know it but he's leading his men to one of the most ornery places there ever was created. They can't turn around and come back down coz the trail ain't wide enough. They gotta keep going.'

'Why are ya so excited?' asked the Kid.

'That trail leads to Satan's Claw,' Red explained.

Palomino raised an eyebrow. 'Where?'

'Ain't ya heard of it?'

'Nope.'

'It's a desert.' Red scratched his crimson whiskers. 'The most back-stabbing desert there ever was. No man can outwit the thing and cross it. It got traps made by the Devil himself in there. Quicksand and acid streams. And sand. A whole heap of sand like ya never seen.'

Kid Palomino shook his head. 'But when they reaches the top and sees the desert they'll turn around and head on back down. Right?'

'Wrong,' Red argued. 'Ain't possible to do that. The trail is even more dangerous coming down than it is going up. And even if ya gets up to the pass between them twin peaks ya can't see the desert for all the trees up on top of that mountain. The only way down is to keep going over the other side on the trail that leads down to the desert. You're halfways down before ya even figures you're in trouble, boy. The other side of that mountain is nothing but weathered rock. Halfway down ya runs out of trees and then all that stands between you and a three-hundred-foot sheer fall is a three-foot-wide trail. One false move and ya takes a mighty long dive. We got them exactly where we wants them, Kid. Now do ya understand?'

'But how are we gonna get them bandits?' Palomino looked even harder at the mountain. 'By my figuring we gotta take the same trail as them. I sure ain't hankering to do that.'

Black Wing made a few gestures and Red chuckled even more loudly as he gathered up his loose reins. 'The Dakota is right. Like me, he knows of a short cut to the desert, which means we don't have to head on up there. We can reach the desert before them varmints manage to come down the other side.'

'A short cut?' Palomino raised an eyebrow. 'To the same desert that ya just told me was full of deadly traps? A shorter route to the place where folks get themselves up and killed. I don't like the sound of that.'

Red reached across and wrapped an arm around his younger friend and squeezed. 'Trust me. I know that desert. I know the safe way round the foot of that mountain right to where an old abandoned adobe mission still stands. Bin there since them Spaniards tried to tame the place.'

'Why did they abandon the mission, Red?' Palomino asked.

'Well, the desert does get kinda hot, boy,' Red ruefully admitted. 'Some say it gets a little too hot even for the good Lord to handle. But if we get to the mission we can use it to give us cover and stop Santiago and his vermin.'

Reluctantly Kid Palomino nodded. 'OK. Let's fill all of our canteens and head on out for that real ornery desert.'

'Satan's Claw,' Red reproved as Black

Wing dropped to the ground and began to fill his water bag.

The Kid dismounted and started to unscrew the stopper of one of his canteens before lowering it into the creek. 'Tell me, Red. How do ya know so much about this Satan's Claw?'

'Got me lost there once.' Red shrugged.

Palomino sighed. 'Figures.'

14

The small natural parapet being used by the bandits had been created countless centuries before when half of the mountain succumbed to the devilish heat of the desert and fell away, crashing into the scorching terrain below.

The horses slowly made their way in line out from the cover of the trees at the top of the mountain and into the blistering sunlight. A heat haze lingered below them as the bandits continued to make their way down towards the golden vastness of the desert. One by one as they descended into the cruel heat the bandits gasped in horror as they saw the blurred reality of what lay below their perilous path.

This was no paradise, as their leader had promised. Santiago had been wrong. Totally wrong. This was hell on earth.

The noise of their horses' hoofs echoed all around them off the sheer rockface. It sounded as though a hundred carpenters were hammering nails into each of their coffins.

Santiago said nothing as his eyes widened and took in the vast desert far below them shimmering in the wavy light of the rising thermals.

His demented brain vainly tried to understand. What had happened to the beautiful land they had ridden through after crossing the Rio Grande? Santiago stopped spurring his white stallion for fear of what he could now see. There was nothing but death for any of the riders if they made one single error.

Again Santiago tried to fathom their plight. Where were the lush green pastures? Where had they gone?

How could there be a desert in the place he had always believed to be Eden? Texas had deserts? His hands gripped his reins tightly as though that offered him safety. The white stallion carefully continued to make its way down the hazardous natural ledge. Santiago slid his sword back into its sheath. This was no place to wield swords. This was a place to try to escape death.

'What is this place, General?' A voice from one of his followers resounded off the rocks.

'I do not like this, General,' Ramon added. He was trying to keep the pack animal he was leading under control as it fought to flee. 'This place is not good.'

'Ramon is right. This place is very bad,' Luis Ruiz shouted out to the man in the fancy tunic, who continued silently to lead them.

Santiago gritted his teeth and tried to control his shaking body so that none of his men might see how scared he actually was. 'Silence, *amigos*. This is the shortest trail to El Paso. Have you not heard of El Paso? There much gold in El Paso and no man has ever attacked that city from this direction. It is all part of my plan. My plan for us to conquer this land.'

A disgruntled chorus of muttering swept along the line of bandits as the riders tried to believe the words they all knew to be nothing but lies.

Ramon was leaning on his left stirrup so that he could turn almost backwards to fight with the terrified packhorse that was tethered to his saddle cantle. 'I am frightened, General.'

'There is nothing to fear,' Santiago yelled out. His words echoed all around the horsemen. 'Be brave.'

Then a chilling sound filled their ears as Ramon lost his battle with the packhorse. His scream resounded all around them as his mount's hoofs slipped on the uneven ledge bringing it to its knees. The packhorse, laden down with bags filled with loot, bucked and charged forwards into Ramon's mount. The bandit felt his saddle slip. His hands feverishly clawed at the very air itself as his fingers tried vainly to reach his saddle horn. The force of the packhorse hitting his already stricken mount sent the bandit hurtling off the saddle. For a moment Ramon thought that he might be safe as his hips hit the edge of the rocky ledge, but then the sunbaked stone crumbled beneath him. Ramon rolled helplessly over until he tumbled off the edge of the precipice. His horse tried to get back to its feet, but it also slipped and fell. All the bandits watched in stunned silence as the packhorse was also dragged to its death. Only a panic-stricken scream remained as the pitiful Ramon and the two horses hurtled downwards and then disappeared into the hot shimmering air far below them.

Each of the bandits sat astride his horse, clutching his reins in drunken terror. A few seconds later they heard the distant sound of three thumps, as each of the creatures stopped falling and hit the desert floor.

Santiago steadied his white mount.

He turned and looked at his stunned men. Then he started to shout at them loudly. 'Let that be a lesson to you all, *amigos*. Be vigilant and brave. Ramon was not and he has paid the price. Do as I command or you will also die as Ramon did. Come. This is no place for stinking cowards. Follow me and you shall all taste the fruits of victory.'

There were no cheers; just silence.

Santiago slapped his reins. The white stallion walked forward once more, while its master tried to look unconcerned at the head of the caravan.

Reluctantly the line of bandits followed.

There was no other way.

15

A wall of heat hit the two deputies and their Indian companion as they closed in on the notorious desert that had probably claimed more lives even than Santiago and his followers over the years. Black Wing led the way on his agile pony as the two deputies kept pace behind him. The trees began to thin out the further the three horsemen rode around the foot of the mountain until only a handful of dying trees stood between them and the strangely shimmering landscape directly ahead of them.

The trail seemed to vanish before them into the waves of hot air. Sand dunes shimmered beneath the blazing sun, whilst a towering wall of rock rose up into the cloudless sky. There was no shelter here in Satan's Claw. This was a place upon which men had long since turned their backs.

Only the Devil himself would have felt at home in this unholy terrain. Unbearable heat seemed to burn the air itself before living creatures had a chance of sucking it into their starved lungs. Yet the three riders pressed on through the last of the cremated vegetation until they saw it. Red and Black Wing had been to this devilish place before but Kid Palomino stared at it with unbelieving eyes.

The sun reflected off the dunes as from a mirror. The blinding light dazzled and confused the riders. The Dakota warrior slowed his mount when the parched earth suddenly turned to lifeless golden sand. Black Wing stopped his pony and leapt to the ground, giving his mount a chance to rest. The Kid and Red drew rein beside him.

The tall Indian pointed to their left.

Palomino screwed up his eyes and tried vainly to see what the Dakota Sioux was indicating.

'I don't see nothing, Red,' the Kid admitted, dragging a sleeve across his sweating brow. 'Nothing but that damn shimmering haze.'

'Me neither, but I sure know what's out there,' Red said. He cast his attention to the wall of rock to his right, which was bathed in bright sunlight. 'Black Wing is telling us the old adobe mission is out there. About a half-mile or maybe closer.'

The Kid eased his palomino stallion to the side of the older man and then looked up at the towering cliff. It was an awesome sight. Then he saw the line of horsemen descending a perilous trail down to the desert floor.

'There they are, Red,' Palomino said, standing in his stirrups. 'Damn it all. You was right about us reaching here before they even got halfway down to the desert floor.'

'Looks like they lost a couple of their bunch by them gaps in the line of horses, Kid,' Red said. He tried to count the exact number of bandits following the man on the white horse. 'I count me about thirty at most.'

Palomino smiled. 'With any luck that wall of rock will thin them out a tad more before we have to fight them.'

No sooner had the words left his lips than a gut-wrenching scream echoed out. Both men watched as a horse and its rider fell from the high trail. The bandit kept on screaming until death greeted him at the base of the cliff.

'Ya might be right, Kid,' Red nodded.

Black Wing made a grunt and aimed his finger to the lead rider upon the white stallion. His hands spoke to Red and the deputy sighed.

'He's seen Santiago, Kid.'

'What's he saying?'

'Our pal here's got killing on his mind, Kid,' Red replied. 'I sure wouldn't wanna be Santiago if Black Wing gets his hands on him.'

'I reckon we all got killing on our minds if the truth was known, Red.' Palomino gave a long sigh.

Red glanced at his friend. 'Not the

kinda killing Black Wing got his heart set on. We're driven by the law about stopping killers. With him it's personal.'

'Revenge,' Kid Palomino agreed. 'By my figuring he got the right though, Red.'

'Sure enough, boy.' Red Rivers moved his quarter horse to the side of the tall Indian and gestured with his hands as he spoke aloud. 'C'mon, Black Wing. We gotta get to the mission and see if it's possible to defend that old place from Santiago.'

'Santiago,' Black Wing said aloud to the surprise of the two deputies.

They both watched as the Indian swung up on to the back of the pony and gathered in the crude rope reins. He turned the head of the animal and thundered away in the direction of the mission.

Palomino turned his horse. 'I sure didn't like the way he said Santiago's name there.'

'Me neither, Kid.'

Both lawmen spurred and chased the

Indian pony out into the burning desert. As they rode they both silently wondered what their comrade had planned for the leader of the bandits. Whatever it was, it would have to be mighty bad to equal the atrocities Santiago had been dishing out.

★ ★ ★

The elegant horse and its master had made good pace across the range of swaying grass in pursuit of Marshal Matt Fallen. The horseman squinted through the afternoon sun at the slow-moving buckboard and the pair of cowboys who were sitting up on its driver's board. Black Boone shortened the distance from the vehicle and the cutting horse tied to its tailgate like a shark closing in on its next meal.

Neither Seth Riley or Pete Hope had heard the approach of the gambler as he stood high in the stirrups and urged his powerful stallion after them. Then the sound of the fine silver adornments which covered the gambler's saddle and bridle drew the attention of both cowboys. Hope held on to the reins of the buckboard and spat as his friend turned round and looked back at the rider.

'Who is it?' Hope hissed.

'It's that damn cardsharp,' Riley answered.

'The varmint that killed old Lou?'

'The same.' Riley pulled his gun from its holster and tried to pull back on its hammer. The gun, like its owner, was in need of lubrication.

Hope glanced at the gun in his companion's hands. 'What in tarnation ya got that hogleg out for, Seth?'

'What ya think? I'm gonna kill him for killing Lou,' Riley snapped back as he eventually managed to get the hammer to lock into position. 'He might have had the law on his side back in town, but he sure ain't got nobody to help him out here.'

Hope lashed the reins down on the backs of the two sturdy horses and tried to get the team to find new pace. 'Are ya loco? That critter shot Lou dead darn easy and he was about sixty feet away from him when he done it.'

Riley ran fingers across the rusted gun in his lap and watched as Boone came ever closer. His eyes wrinkled up as he stared at the flamboyant horseman.

'I'm gonna kill him and leave his stinking carcass out here for the coyotes to feast on.'

'That's loco talk,' Hope told him. 'Boone will kill ya like a dog if'n he sees that gun. Put it away.'

Boone closed in on the buckboard. 'Hold on there,' he called.

'Stop this buckboard, Pete,' Riley told his friend. 'Soon as he draws level I'll blow his head clean off.'

Hope lashed the reins down on the team again. 'I ain't gonna stop and have ya shooting at that bastard. He'll kill ya for sure.'

'Stop.' Riley tried to drag the reins from Hope's hands.

'Nope. He'll kill ya,' Hope shouted as the gambler rode to the buckboard's lead horse and grabbed its bridle. Boone leaned back and the team slowed.

Boone looked back at the cowboys. 'Stop this thing. I want to talk with you.'

There was a look in Black Boone's face which scared Hope right down to the holes in his longjohns. He pushed a boot down on the brake pole and then eased the reins back. The buckboard was brought to a halt amid the tall grass.

Boone turned his horse and walked it around the stationary vehicle as he inspected it with his narrowed eyes. He ignored the coffin on the flatbed and eased his black horse up next to Hope.

'Ya partner figuring on using that gun?' Boone asked Hope, while keeping his eyes on Riley.

Hope said nothing.

Black Boone stood in his stirrups and smiled coldly at Seth Riley. 'Well?

Either shoot me or holster that before I kill you.'

'Ya killed Lou,' Riley snarled. He raised the gun and waved it at the gambler. 'Now I'm gonna kill you, Boone. An eye for an eye.'

Before Riley had even stroked the gun's trigger, Boone had drawn and fired his own .44. A white flash preceded the deafening bullet which exploded from the barrel of the well-notched weapon. The shot hit the cowboy dead centre. Riley flew backwards off the buckboard and crashed into the ground.

Pete Hope steadied the alarmed team with both hands and watched fearfully as the gambler rode around the vehicle to stare down at his handiwork.

'Self-defence. Right?' Boone smiled as he looked at the cowboy.

Hope nodded. 'Right enough. Seth was gonna kill ya right enough. That was self-defence. No doubt about it. I'll be happy to tell Marshal Fallen that Seth drew first.'

Boone suddenly looked all around them. 'Where is the good marshal, friend?'

Hope pointed a shaking arm to where smoke still rose up into the afternoon sky. 'He went to find out about that smoke, Boone.'

The gambler sighed. 'Interesting. At least I know which direction he went.'

Pete Hope could feel the sweat trailing down from the band of his hat. It stung his eyes. 'Don't ya go fretting none. I'll tell the marshal that this was self-defence. No problem.'

Boone returned his attention to the man holding the reins in his hands. 'The trouble is you might change your mind and tell the law a different story. I ain't hankering to have my neck stretched on the word of a grubby little cowpoke.'

'I wouldn't change my mind, Boone,' Hope insisted.

Black Boone thought for a while, then clawed the hammer back on his gun again. With an icy stare he looked at the cowboy and then squeezed the trigger. The shot cut through the afternoon air and caught the cowboy in the head. Both of Hope's hands released their grip on the reins as his body was sent tumbling off the high driver's seat. The startled team of horses stampeded away from the sound of the ear-splitting shot with their buckboard in tow.

Without a hint of any emotion Boone removed the spent casings from his smoking gun and replaced them with fresh bullets. He holstered his gun on his left hip and pulled a silver cigar case from his inside pocket. He smiled to himself.

'Problem solved.'

Boone struck a match on his silver saddle horn and raised its flame to a long thin cigar. He inhaled the smoke deeply and tossed the match aside.

The gambler swung his elegant horse round, tapped his spurs and headed to where the black smoke still twisted its way upward from what remained of Sweet Water.

The horseman stood in his stirrups and silently continued his search for Matt Fallen.

16

Rolling waves of golden sand stretched all the way from the base of the mountain to the weathered mission and beyond: a dead land amid so much fertile terrain. Poisoned by creeks of acidic liquid that seeped up from volcanic lakes far below the desolate desert, and with areas of deadly dry quicksand, Satan's Claw had earned a reputation for killing everything that dared to venture upon its wastes. It was an ocean of sand that, in its own way, was just as dangerous as anything found beyond any coastline. The adobe mission had not fared well in the harsh, unforgiving climate of Satan's Claw. It was obvious to the three horsemen as they dismounted why the monks had abandoned the once imposing structure and fled to greener pastures.

More than a hundred years before it

must have been obvious that nothing could flourish in this arid landscape. No amount of praying could turn this into anything other than a graveyard of bleached bones.

This was a desert where life and death constantly battled and death was usually the winner. Things tended to die in Satan's Claw.

Red Rivers tied all three of their mounts close to the highest point in the ancient construction: its once impressive bell tower. Even he had to admit that the remote mission was only half as big as it had been the last time he had been here. Walls had fallen in the meantime as the sun sucked the last of the moisture from the adobe bricks.

Back then it could have been defended easily but not now.

The weary men rested for a few moments as they studied the place more seriously. For all its degradation, it still had one thing going for it; one vital element was in its favour, and that was its situation.

This mission was like the Alamo. Perfectly placed to slow up or even stop any who tried to advance deeper into Texas. Set between mountain and everything beyond, the crumbling structure was the only place capable of hindering Santiago's bloody advance.

Red Rivers knew that anyone who had travelled down from the mountain trail had to pass this point in the otherwise featureless desert. This was where Santiago and his small army could be halted and hopefully destroyed.

Yet time had not been kind to the mission. Its once high walls had crumbled until there was barely any sign of them in the hot sand that had encroached into what had once been a courtyard. The monks' cells had once been sturdy but not even they had survived the ravages of the desert and the sun. Apart from the front wall and most of a bell tower, virtually all of the rest of the once impressive building had returned to dust. The back walls of the mission had simply eroded until they were barely two feet high.

Kid Palomino swallowed hard and strode to the centre of the courtyard. He looked at what had once been a deep well. He rested his hands on the edge of the well and looked into the void. He sighed, then rubbed his neck. If there had been water in the well there was no sign of it now.

'Just as I figured. This well is full of sand,' the Kid told his companions. 'Good job we filled all our canteens.'

'Ain't got time to fret over that, boy,' Red said, pointing his red beard at the mountain. 'Look. Them bandits are almost down.'

Palomino checked his guns, stared through the wavy atmosphere and saw the white horse as it led the others to the sand. He then spun on his heels and joined Red, who was standing beside their horses beneath the bell tower. Red secured the reins of the three animals and rubbed his jaw.

'This sure ain't how it was, boy,' he said. 'This place has just fallen down like an old woodwormed outhouse.'

'It can be defended though. Right?' Palomino asked.

'Maybe.' Red led the younger deputy up adobe steps until they were inside the almost square tower. The roof and rear wall had long gone but the walls halfway up the adobe structure remained intact, offering cover on three sides. Two holes were all that remained of shuttered windows. Both men stared out and could see the bandit leader's white stallion as it approached the floor of the desert.

'Damn it all. Santiago has reached the foot of the cliff, Red?' the Kid exclaimed. 'Once the rest of them critters join him I figure we got maybe five minutes at best before they reach here. Unless they take a different course.'

'There ain't no other way for them varmints to head except here, Kid,' Red told him drily. 'They don't have no knowledge of the trail that'll lead them back to Sweet Water.'

Palomino took a deep breath. 'Reckon they'll get here real fast once their horses got their second wind. Ain't hardly no distance between there and here. We got maybe five minutes at most to get ourselves bedded down to fend them off.'

Red gave a sly grin. 'Or maybe a tad longer.'

'How'd ya mean?' Palomino asked.

'That sand ain't like most sand ya knows of, Kid.' Red led his pal back down to their horses. 'It's riddled with patches of quicksand.'

Kid Palomino thought about the statement for a while as his friend dragged his Winchester from the saddle scabbard. 'Quicksand? Are ya sure?'

'Yep.' Red lifted the flap of one of his saddle-bag satchels and pulled out two boxes of rifle bullets. He tossed one to his friend. 'I'm dead sure, Kid. Lost me a mighty fine horse in that stuff last time I was here.'

'We might have us a fighting chance,' Palomino said.

'A slim 'un, anyways,' Red corrected.

Both men looked at the Dakota warrior. Black Wing was crouched down, glaring out into the haze at the mountain a mere quarter of a mile away from the front of the mission. There was a grim expression carved into his handsome features. One which both men had seen many times before.

It was the look of revenge as it filtered through every sinew of the warrior's being. Black Wing had only one thing he had to do, and that was avenge his people. It was a fiery fever which only killing those who had killed his family could extinguish. Nothing else mattered to the brave Dakota.

'Black Wing,' Palomino called out across the twenty feet which separated them. The Indian showed no sign of hearing the young deputy. He just kept watching the bandits as they slowly gathered around their leader.

'I got me a feeling he could do more killing with that bow of his than we could do with all our guns and rifles, Red,' the Kid said.

Red nodded. 'Yep. If'n he's like the rest of his people's warriors he'll not miss an awful lot with that bow.'

Kid Palomino placed a hand on the wooden stock of his rifle and pulled it clear of the saddle. He cocked its mechanism and sent a spent casing flying over his shoulder. 'How many boxes of ammunition we got, Red?'

'Enough to last us,' Red answered. 'As long as we don't last too long.'

Palomino looked all around them. Few places could have been harder to defend than the remains of what they now stood in. The mission was not what he had imagined when Red had told him of its existence. He knew that once it must have been as solid as any fortress ever constructed, but now it was a mere shadow of its former self. At one time this place might have been capable of keeping an army at bay. Not any longer. Apart from the front wall to either side of what had once been the gateway into the courtyard, and the tower, the rest was just a memory.

'The only place we got a chance of not getting shot full of holes is up in the bell tower,' the Kid said.

Red gave a nod. 'You're right. I sure wish that tower still had four walls instead of just three, though.'

Black Wing rose to his full imposing height, glanced at both deputies, then spoke silently with his hands.

'They've all reached the desert floor,' Red told Palomino.

'How many?'

Again Black Wing addressed the pair of lawmen with hand gestures.

'He counted twenty-five,' Red interpreted.

Kid Palomino was thoughtful. 'Still an awful lot of bandits, Red. Ya figure we can handle them?'

'Hell. Who gives a damn?' Red joked. 'We ain't got nothing else to do, have we?'

Without warning Black Wing ran across the courtyard to the three horses. Like a puma he leapt up on to his pony's back, dragged the rope rein free and rode out into the dunes of sand. He was heading to the east of the high mountain.

Both men watched as the Dakota warrior galloped into the shimmering haze. Within seconds both pony and master had vanished from sight.

'Where's he going?' Palomino asked his partner. 'That ain't the direction them bandits are. I don't get it.'

Red rubbed his whiskers. 'He's circling them, boy. Like a mountain lion circles a grazing critter before he strikes. He's going up wind of them.'

'Sure wish he'd stuck around.' For the first time in his life Kid Palomino doubted their ability to win a fight. He wondered whether he and his friend had bitten off too much.

Too much for even them to swallow.

'Twenty-five, he said,' Red mumbled. 'Bad odds. Even for us that's mighty bad odds, Kid.'

The Kid sighed and started to go up into the tower again. 'C'mon. Like ya said. We ain't got nothing else to do.'

As the last of the bandits finished their long trek down the perilous pathway into Satan's Claw Santiago Del Rosa stared blankly at the bodies of his fallen men and their horses, lying dead at the bottom of the steep, jagged cliff. There was not a hint of any emotion in his face as his brutal mind tried to work out what he should do in order to get them out of this baking-hot desert.

So far Santiago had managed to maintain his control over the band of death-dealing bandits with little more than vague promises and bravado. Now the cunning Santiago knew that he would have to try to make good on all of those pledges if he were to survive as their leader unchallenged.

Santiago looked at the nearest of his beleaguered men. He pointed at the broken bodies of the dead men and horses.

'Hurry. Collect all the saddle-bags from our dead *amigos* and share the loot in them between you,' the bandit leader ordered. 'Their misfortune is your gain.'

The men did as Santiago had instructed and scrambled over the bloodstained rocks to the lifeless bodies.

Only Luis Ruiz remained beside the tall white horse as Santiago stared out into the shimmering heat haze.

'What do you see, General?' he asked as he dismounted.

'I am not sure, Luis,' Santiago admitted. He walked further away from his men as they plundered the dead of all their possessions. 'There seems to be something out there. Do you see it, *amigo*?'

Luiz stepped to the side of Santiago, raised his hand against the blinding sun and stared out into the heart of the desert, beyond the rolling dunes.

'*Sí*. I see something.'

Santiago leaned towards his most loyal follower. 'But what do you see, Luis? Do you see a vision of a fortress, as I do?'

Luis nodded. '*Sí*. It is a fortress. But

what would such a thing be doing in the middle of a desert? There is no need for soldiers out here.'

The leader of the bandits took another step into the soft, burning sand. He squinted even harder. A crooked smile crossed his face and he clapped his hands together. 'Wait. I think it is not a fortress but a castle. A golden castle with a tower. Is it not so?'

Again Luis agreed. '*Sí*, General. A mighty fortress made from bricks of gold. Look how it shines. It is ours for the taking.'

Santiago removed his sombrero and threw it up into the air. He was elated. 'Luis. We have found the most precious thing in all of Texas. We have found a castle made from gold.'

'And it is ours.' Luis smiled.

Santiago turned to his men and raised both arms. They all looked at their joyous leader with stunned weary eyes.

'Stop stealing the teeth from the dead ones, *amigos*. We have something far more precious awaiting us out there.

Mount up and I shall lead you all to a castle made from gold.'

Pedro staggered towards his brother and Santiago. He, like every one of the bandits, needed water and food.

'The men need rest, General,' Pedro said.

'There is no time to rest, Pedro,' Santiago shouted. 'There is a castle made of gold out there. Are you blind? Do you not see it?'

'I see only a mud-brick adobe,' Pedro sighed.

Santiago was furious. 'It is a golden castle.'

'What is this madness, General?' Pedro gasped. 'We are tired and we need to make camp and eat and rest. What are you saying about castles made of gold?'

'You dare to argue with Santiago?'

Total exhaustion had not slowed any of the bandit leader's abilities. With the speed of a striking sidewinder Santiago drew his sword and slashed Pedro. The blade went deep into the chest and belly of the bandit. Too deep for any man to survive. Pedro shook as his innards spilled out from the terrifying wound.

'Pedro?' gasped a horrified Luis. He watched his brother fall to his knees as gore flowed from him. Pedro then fell on to his face at the feet of Santiago.

Santiago watched the blood dripping from his sword then turned to Luis. 'More gold for us, *amigo*.'

'But Pedro was my brother, General,' Luis Ruiz said. 'You have killed my brother.'

Santiago grabbed the reins of his horse, stepped into his stirrup and mounted the tall stallion. 'As I shall kill anyone who dares to argue with me. Come.'

The bandits staggered to their horses and started to mount as Santiago drove his spurs into the flesh of his horse and rode out into the dunes. Within a mere heartbeat the others were blindly following.

Palomino was first to spot the advancing riders. He lifted his rifle and brought it up to his shoulder. Then suddenly a barrage of bullets rained in on the adobe as the bandits noticed the two men vainly attempting to defend it. Chunks of mud brick shattered under the fusillade and showered over the Kid and Red as they blasted their carbines in reply.

Even more bullets ripped through the haze from the guns of the galloping bandits.

'Damn, they sure got good eyesight,' Red groaned from under a blanket of adobe dust.

'Quit gabbing,' yelled the Kid over the deafening sound of gunplay.

Santiago stopped his mount as two of his men were punched off their saddles by the powerful rifle bullets. Totally surprised by the unexpected gunfire Santiago called out to his men to halt but only two close to him heard his command. The rest kept on galloping towards the distant mission with their weaponry blasting.

'What is happening, General?' one of

the bandits close to Santiago screamed out. 'Who is shooting at us?'

Santiago did not reply. Utterly confused, he stared hard through the heat haze at the adobe. His heart sank.

'It is not gold,' Santiago whispered to himself. 'It is mud.'

Seeing his men falling as bullets cut them from their saddles Santiago swung his mighty stallion round and stared at the only two riders who had obeyed his orders and stopped. The others had charged on with their guns blazing.

Looking at the terrified pair of bandits, Santiago raised his sword. Then he felt the long weapon being ferociously ripped from his grip. The bandit stared in disbelief as his sword flew to the baking-hot sand. The two bandits beside him gasped as he lowered his arm and stared at the warm blood dripping from his hand. To his horror Santiago's hand had been skewered by a black arrow which was still embedded between the bone and muscle.

'Who dares do this to Santiago?' he screamed out. Then he heard the sound of two more arrows as they passed within inches of him.

His head turned just as the two riders beside him jolted back on their saddles before falling to the ground. Santiago eyed the bodies. Both had been hit by lethal black arrows. Arrows identical to the one still in his hand.

The air was thick with the acrid scent of gunsmoke. Santiago was trying to pull the arrow free when another flew into his leg. The bandit leader buckled as he gave out a pitiful yell. He grabbed his reins and turned his horse. Then he saw his remaining charging bandits stopping in their tracks. He glared as their horses began to sink into the sand.

One by one they were engulfed.

'What is this magic?' Santiago asked himself. He managed to spin his white stallion round just as Luis disappeared from view, the very sand appearing to consume the bandit. 'What is happening?'

The bandit leader watched as his men followed their horses and sank into the quicksand. Santiago held his reins with his injured hand and turned the mighty horse and spurred. Pain tore through every fibre of his body as both arrows in him mercilessly tore at his bloodied flesh.

The powerful stallion galloped away from the carnage in response to its master's spurs. The mountain loomed over them as they retreated from the incessant salvo of shots ringing out behind them.

Santiago kept spurring and headed back to where he had left the dead bandits lying at the base of the cliff.

By the time he had reached his goal the white mane of the horse had turned red with its master's blood. Then, at last, Santiago realized that the bullets from the adobe mission were falling short. He had managed to drive his horse beyond the range of the Winchesters.

A cloud of gunsmoke swept before Santiago as he eased his horse to a stop.

His blurred eyes looked at the arrow in his thigh. He released the reins, grabbed the shaft of black wood and pulled the arrow out of his leg. A fountain of blood squirted out over the already soiled horse. Santiago ignored it and tried to think.

Then he heard a deep voice saying his name.

'Santiago.'

The bandit leader looked up and saw the Dakota warrior, who was standing just in front of his pony. Black Wing held his bow in one hand whilst his other hovered above the quiver of black arrows.

Suddenly Santiago knew who he was looking at. The warrior was dressed exactly like those he and his men had slaughtered before they had crossed over into Texas.

'Another filthy Indian for me to kill.' Santiago spat and then realized that he had left his trusty sword out on the dunes far behind him. Balancing on the stallion's wide back the injured bandit pulled one of his guns from its holster with his left hand and defiantly cocked its hammer. 'You do not frighten Santiago Del Rosa, *amigo*. I shall kill you like I killed all of your tribe. I shall then spit on your carcass.'

Black Wing did not move a muscle as his hooded eyes remained steady on the bandit.

'You think you are faster than Santiago with that bow?'

The Dakota remained like a statue.

'Say something, you dog.'

Black Wing remained silent.

Furiously Santiago raised the gun and aimed it at the unflinching Indian. 'Now you will die.'

There was a slight movement from Black Wing. So fast that the bandit did not even see what happened next. It was the only clue to the fact that the warrior had primed and fired his deadly arrow straight into the throat of the bandit.

Santiago felt as though he were drowning. He was. Drowning in his own blood. His eyes rolled and he fell from his high perch and landed in the soft sand.

Black Wing silently walked to where Santiago lay and kicked the gun from the lifeless hand. Then turned back to his pony. He grabbed its mane and threw himself up on to the animal's back and gave out a chilling cry.

Back in the mission tower Palomino and Red had watched in stunned silence as each of the bandits had lost their desperate fight and had finally sunk into the quicksand.

Neither deputy felt any satisfaction. Only relief.

The Kid rose and looked out across the sun-bleached sand. He turned to his pal.

'Is it over?' he asked.

Red nodded. 'Reckon so.'

'What about that Santiago critter?' Palomino queried. 'I didn't see any white horse sink out there in that sand, Red.'

'Black Wing.' Red said the name and

then started down the steps back to the courtyard with his young friend on his tail.

'What about Black Wing?' the Kid asked.

Red stopped by the wall and rested a shoulder against its crumbling surface. 'He killed Santiago.'

'How'd ya know that?'

Red pointed out to the desert. Black Wing was riding back to the mission. 'He'd sure not have come back here if'n he hadn't killed that bastard, boy.'

Palomino nodded. 'Reckon you're right.'

The Dakota warrior stopped the pony as he reached the gate of the old mission and then spoke to Red with his hands. Red nodded and watched as Black Wing swung his pony round and thundered back into the shimmering haze.

'What he tell ya, Red?'

'He told me he done what he had to do,' Red answered. 'I don't reckon he liked the way it made him feel though, Kid.'

'Revenge is a bitter pill to swallow.' Palomino nodded.

'Yep. Mighty bitter.'

Kid Palomino stepped out into the bright sunlight and looked in the direction from which they had ridden to the mission. He pointed a finger and smiled.

'Don't look now, but Marshal Fallen's heading here, Red.'

The older deputy glanced at the familiar rider with the gleaming tin star pinned to his vest.

'Now ain't that just the worst timing ya ever done seen, Palomino?' Red laughed.

The big man on the cowboy horse rode up to the adobe and drew rein beside the two men. Fallen stared out at the desert and the bodies which still remained on the hot sand.

'That was a mighty fine show you boys put on there,' said the marshal. 'I caught sight of it as I cleared that brush yonder. By the time I had reached the dunes it was all over.'

'If ya had used them spurs of yours you might have bin able to join in, Marshal.' Red grinned.

Fallen patted the shoulder of the wily deputy.

Finale

The sky was filled with a myriad stars as the three lawmen rode along the dry riverbed beneath a canopy of tree branches. To both sides high grass fringed wide rocks. A mile or so ahead they knew they would reach the high range once more and be on their way back to War Smoke.

Fallen rode between the two deputies as slowly their horses climbed a slight ridge. Cutting up between a handful of trees the trio reached the range and eased back on their reins. The horses stopped and the riders rested.

The half-moon cast its light across the top of the swaying grass as all three dismounted and allowed their mounts to eat their fill of the sweet grass. To their right a large smooth boulder, taller than a house, dominated the entire area.

Fallen could see the distant dots of light that he knew to be War Smoke. 'Can't wait to get back home.'

'Ya miss it?' Palomino asked.

'Not really. I'm kinda used to it, though,' Fallen answered as he looked all around them.

'Something troubling you, Marshal?' the Kid asked.

Fallen looked at both men. 'For the last mile or so I've had this feeling we're being watched, Kid.'

Red nodded and slid his tongue along the gummed edge of a cigarette paper. 'Now that's strange. I had me the same inkling, Marshal.'

'Reckon I must be just tired.' Fallen shrugged. 'Ain't slept in a couple of nights.'

'Too tired to draw that long-barrelled Colt, Marshal?'

The three lawmen froze to the spot as the familiar voice of the gambler washed over them. Kid Palomino had instinctively drawn both his guns when he heard Black Boone's voice come from beside the huge rock.

'Holster them guns, Kid,' Fallen ordered. 'He don't want you. He wants me.'

Reluctantly Kid Palomino dropped both his .45s back into their hand-tooled holsters.

Fallen remained calm. He stepped away from both his men and their horses, towards the moonlit rock. He kept walking until he could see the lean elegant figure who stood beside it.

Fallen paused. 'Boone.'

'I want you to know that this ain't personal, Marshal,' Boone said as he pushed his coat tail over the gun on his hip. 'This is business.'

The marshal turned to face the man who had been paid to kill him. He could not conceal his confusion.

'I don't understand. What ya mean?' Fallen asked.

'I've been paid to kill you, Marshal,' Boone told him. 'A thousand dollars for taking you out of the picture.'

Fallen squared up to the gambler.

'Who paid you to kill me, Boone? Who?'

Black Boone stepped away from the boulder and flexed his fingers. 'I can't go telling you that. That's a private matter between me and the man who wants you dead. You understand?'

Palomino made a slight movement but Fallen raised a large hand. 'You stay where ya are, Kid. This ain't nothing to do with you. This is my problem.'

'I ain't gonna let that varmint gun ya down, Marshal,' the Kid announced.

'He won't, Palomino,' Fallen said drily.

Boone grinned. 'I'm faster than you and I'm gonna prove it, Marshal.'

'I'm waiting.' Fallen sighed. His hand hovered over his holstered Colt.

Both men went for their guns. Boone had drawn, cocked and fired before the marshal's gun had cleared its holster. Fallen felt his hip jerk to the side as the bullet cut through the leather and severed the holster from its belt.

A stunned Matt Fallen felt the

holstered gun fall to the ground down by his boots. His eyes looked at the smiling gambler, who was holding his smoking .44 in his hand.

'I told you I was faster than you, Marshal,' Boone said. He turned the gun toward the deputies. 'Now unhitch your belts and let them drop, boys. I'll kill Fallen if you don't.'

'Do as he says, boys,' Fallen instructed.

Both Red and Palamino unbuckled their gunbelts and let them drop to the ground.

'Excellent.' Boone came a step closer and aimed his gun at the tall marshal. He paused again, raised the Colt and aimed straight at Fallen's head. 'Now it will be easy for me to kill you all in turn.'

Matt Fallen's eyes narrowed. 'It's me you've been paid to kill, Boone. Not them. Let them be.'

'How?' Boone's thumb pulled back on the gun's hammer until it locked. 'I have to kill them when I've killed you. I can't leave witnesses, can I?'

Suddenly out of the darkness came a noise. The noise of an arrow in flight. A black arrow.

Boone heard it just before the lethal projectile thumped into his chest. Stunned, the gambler staggered back a few steps as another identical arrow hit him in the neck. He fell backwards and crashed into the ground. The .44 discharged its bullet up into the heavens. The gun fell from the dead man's hand.

Matt Fallen rushed to the body, then looked at the two deputies in surprise.

'What happened? I don't understand,' the bewildered marshal gasped. 'Who did this?'

Kid Palomino picked up his gunbelt and strapped it round his hips again. 'Take it easy, Marshal. We'll explain on the way back to War Smoke.'

Marshal Fallen marched back to the two deputies. 'Explain what?'

'Explain about Black Wing, Marshal,' Palamino told him.

'Who?'

Red Rivers scooped up his gunbelt and looked out into the darkness. He smiled. For a tantalizing moment he thought he saw the Dakota warrior raise his arms in salute to them.

'What ya looking at, Red?' Fallen asked the old deputy.

'Just an old friend, Marshal,' Red answered with a sigh.

We do hope that you have enjoyed reading this large print book.

Did you know that all of our titles are available for purchase?

We publish a wide range of high quality large print books including:
Romances, Mysteries, Classics
General Fiction
Non Fiction and Westerns

Special interest titles available in large print are:
The Little Oxford Dictionary
Music Book, Song Book
Hymn Book, Service Book

Also available from us courtesy of Oxford University Press:
Young Readers' Dictionary
(large print edition)
Young Readers' Thesaurus
(large print edition)

For further information or a free brochure, please contact us at:
Ulverscroft Large Print Books Ltd.,
The Green, Bradgate Road, Anstey,
Leicester, LE7 7FU, England.
Tel: (00 44) **0116 236 4325**
Fax: (00 44) **0116 234 0205**

Other titles in the
Linford Western Library:

LADY COLT

Steve Hayes

When word comes through that two of the infamous Wallace brothers have been spotted in Indian Territory, Liberty Mercer — only the second woman ever to become a Deputy US Marshal — rides out to arrest them. But things don't go to plan, and Liberty finds herself left in the desert to die. Fortunately, rescue comes in the unlikely shape of a young girl named Clementina, on the run herself — from a stepmother who happens to be the matriarch of the Wallace gang . . .

THE GHOSTS OF POYNTER

Amos Carr

Chase Tyler is headed for the town of Poynter. An attempted ambush, the death of an innocent man and a sheriff who won't play by the rules, added to a brother-in-law who can't be trusted and a young man out for vengeance, all make for a pretty complicated visit. When Chase also meets a woman who bears more than a passing resemblance to his lost love, it would seem there is very little hope of him laying old ghosts to rest . . .

STOP OLLINGER!

Jack Dakota

When the town of Mud Wagon Creek is destroyed by desperadoes, it is just the start of a twisted trail of revenge for outlaw-boss Bass Ollinger. He has sworn to make society pay for the time he spent in the Oregon State Penitentiary, and he intends to blaze a trail of death and destruction clear from Texas to the Beaver State ... Riding the border country, Brant Forrest unwittingly rides into Ollinger's path, and comes to the inevitable conclusion: stop Ollinger!

ACE OF BONES

Clay Starmer

When famed gunslinger Reno Valance rides out, the instructions are clear: collect his wife's relative and return home. But for the man who used to be known as Ace, it turns out not to be so simple: Uncle Gifford is dead — murdered! Soon a world of evil is unleashed, and Reno is forced to make a decision. He's dealt the devil's card for twenty years, and now he'll have to do it once more, taking up his Remington as the Ace of Bones . . .

BEYOND REDEMPTION

I. J. Parnham

As a child, Jeff Dale witnesses the terrible aftermath of an atrocity: Elmer Drake has killed three members of a family, but the daughter, Cynthia, is missing. Jeff vows that he'll find her, no matter how long it takes. Years later, after finding a clue about Cynthia's fate, Jeff follows the trail to the frontier town of Redemption. Here stalks a man who carries a gun in one hand and a cross in the other. A man called Elmer Drake . . .